"Rachel...?"

Garrett's voice was oddly gentle, breaking in on their shared silence, the soft music of the running stream, the creak of the porch swing.

Turning her head slightly, Rachel found him gazing at her.

"Would you take off your clothes?"

Her heart gave just the tiniest lurch. "What did you say?"

"Take off your clothes. I want to see you naked in the moonlight. I want to touch you, take you onto my lap...." His voice was growing deeper, husky. "I want you right here, right now.... I want to be inside you...."

He was making love to her with words. Only words. Rachel felt a spreading warmth in her groin, felt it creep like gossamer threads of fire until it encompassed her entire being. "You're crazy," she whispered, even as her fingers trembled at the buttons of her blouse.

Books by Jackie Weger

HARLEQUIN TEMPTATION

HARLEQUIN AMERICAN ROMANCE

These books may be available at your local bookseller.

Don't miss any of our special offers. Write to us at the following address for information on our newest releases.

Harlequin Reader Service
P.O. Box 52040, Phoenix, AZ 85072-2040
Canadian address: P.O. Box 2800, Postal Station A,
5170 Yonge St., Willowdale, Ont. M2N 6J3

The Wings of Morning

JACKIE WEGER

Harlequin Books

TORONTO • NEW YORK • LONDON
AMSTERDAM • PARIS • SYDNEY • HAMBURG
STOCKHOLM • ATHENS • TOKYO • MILAN

For
Marj Gurasich

Published January 1986

ISBN 0-373-25189-0

Printed in Canada

1

"ARE YOU STILL PRETTY, MAMA?"

Rachel closed her eyes tightly, shutting out the stove, the canner, the jars of tomatoes, the air in the kitchen that was like sweat-dampened silk that clings to skin on a humid day. Was she still pretty? Had she ever been? *Yes!* she thought defiantly. But she must have let herself go these past five months if her nine-year-old was raising the question. Rachel opened her eyes and faced her son. He was slim and wiry, his nose speckled with freckles, and it would be years before he grew into his ears. His shorts were dark around the waist with perspiration and his thin shoulders were bent with the weight of the basket he had hauled from the garden. He looked so solemn her smile died on her lips. "Whatever makes you ask a question like that, Pete?"

He began to sort tomatoes from the basket. "I was just thinking that if you were still pretty, maybe— maybe you could find another daddy to take care of us." He had that hesitant look about his narrow pinched face that suggested he wanted to say more, but Rachel's mouth fell open in astonishment and her reaction preoccupied him.

"Find another... Oh, sweetheart, that's not why people get married."

Pete's ears turned bright red. He averted his face. "I don't see why not. It seems a good reason to me. I can't do it all, Mama. I know you said I was the man of the house now, but I can't do it by myself. If Daddy couldn't . . ." His knotty little Adam's apple bobbed. "I'm sick of tomatoes!"

Rachel grasped the back of a chair, her lungs seeming to constrict and then expand deeply to compensate. *If daddy couldn't . . .* She felt a sharp stab of guilt and disloyalty of the heart. Those late-night arguments about work, Clive's lack of it; money, the lack of it. Arguments she didn't want to remember. "I never meant that you had to, Pete . . ." She could not go on and look at him at the same time, so she turned back to the stove. "I only meant that we all have to pitch in to make a go of it now. You, me, Caroline, even Sara."

"But you said I was the man. I'm not a man, I'm just a little boy."

Rachel's throat went dry. Oh, she had gone about her grief, the children's grief, all wrong. All these months Pete must have been worrying, taking the weight of the world—their world anyway—on himself. She had spoken bravely to make him brave, to make him strong—to make herself feel strong. Now she was learning she had failed dismally.

"I know," she told him softly and waved a hand toward the old scarred kitchen counter. "Look, we've done up sixty jars today. Why don't you take that basket of tomatoes and feed them to your pig. He needs fattening up if he's to take a ribbon at the county fair in the fall. Besides, I don't think I could peel another tomato if my life depended on it. Take a break. Go for a swim in the creek, check on your fish trap. Caroline's down there already, isn't she? And when this batch of canning I've got started is finished, Sara and I'll come down, too."

Pete's gray eyes, so like his father's had been, brightened. "You're sure?"

"I've never been more sure of anything in my life. I need a swim myself, and I'll bring some sandwiches. We can have a picnic."

Turning, dragging the basket hesitantly, Pete just couldn't let go. "Are you sure about the tomatoes? We'll have enough to eat this winter?"

Fighting the lump rising in her throat, Rachel realized that all the things she had said so easily, so glibly— comments about money, food, shelter—Pete had taken hard. "We'll have enough. I'm going to teach this year when school starts, remember?"

"You got the contract! And you didn't tell me?"

"No, no. Not yet, but it'll come as soon as the school board meets. Now scoot. The longer you keep me chatting here, the longer it'll take me to get to that swim."

Rachel listened for the thump-thump of the basket being dragged down the steps, then went to the door and stood there, looking into the distance.

The green Ozark mountains appeared limpid, crowding one another as if they couldn't raise their backs in the oppressive July heat. The thick pine forest that grew on the hills and clung tenaciously to dizzy ravines appeared a hazy blue-green. *You get ideas*, Rachel thought, *you get hopes, you save them up over your life and then . . . reality!*

Her gaze shifted to the clearing. Reality was sparse grass, chickens pecking languidly—chickens bought only that spring as day-old chicks and still too young yet to produce an egg. Reality was the old station wagon needing its flat tire changed. Reality was the old house, its porch unpainted, left corner leaning downward toward the encroaching gully as it had for as long as she could remember. The worst reality of all, though, was loneliness. The kind of loneliness that was buried bone deep, the kind of loneliness that meant a whole dream ended.

She had worked long and hard to get away from this tumble-down house, this constricted life, the succession of dreary tasks. Yet here she was again. The path leading from this house perched on the lonely bluff had been a treacherous circle marked by a college scholarship, a teaching certificate, ten years of marriage and death.

On the other hand, she couldn't discount the fact that the house was now a refuge, never mind the unending chores. Things could be worse. They had been worse. When she and the children had lived in Hickory Grove, every time she left the house she had had to grit her teeth against the thoughts that she knew were behind the open faces of her neighbors, against hesitant words of sympathy.

All she had ever wanted, Rachel told herself, was to touch life, to be surrounded by it. Anything but this. She hugged herself, suffering a moment of quiet ferocity until the canner began to steam and hiss. A small laugh escaped her as she emerged from her thoughts. Never a dull moment! Every hour of every day was spent in survival. She'd make it somehow. She wasn't afraid of hard work, she wasn't afraid of life—not for herself—even if that life was now confined to twenty acres of soaring pine and an old house that was little more than a shabby sentinel of the mountain's privacy.

But what mattered the house? Blackberries grew in great plump profusion along the creek, chipmunks hid beneath the leaf mold and wild red squirrels scolded from overhanging limbs. It was a good clean place to raise her children. Anyway, nothing mattered at the moment but the fact that the tomatoes were almost finished and in ten minutes she would be in White Hawk Creek, the lovely part where the wind-bent chokecherry tree cast its shade over the water, forming a green amphitheater.

THE WATER WAS SHALLOW, coming up to Rachel's knees. Sitting on the sandy bottom, she leaned back on her arms, letting the creek's clear swift flow brush the back of her neck. Where the sun found passage through overhead foliage it shimmered on the creek's rippling surface. She wore shorts that billowed with the current and an old blouse tied beneath her breasts. The children wore only shorts, although seven-year-old Caroline was beginning to be uncomfortable without her blouse. Sweet cynical Caroline. This was her last year of freedom. Rachel had hoped to give her more years, many more. The sound of Sara's silvery laughter caught Rachel's attention. She turned to study her youngest child.

Sara was four, a cherub. Short stubby legs, dark curls framing her round innocent face, a face that hid everything, huge saucer eyes that watched, absorbing all that she saw. Sara communicated to trees, to flowers, to vegetables in the garden, to the chickens, to her dolls, but she wouldn't speak to people. At first, Rachel had been heartsick that her youngest couldn't speak, until last year when she had heard Sara singing, forming words in a soft pure voice. All the doctors who had ever seen Sara insisted she would talk when she was ready. Ready! Rachel shook her head in exasperation. Not once had she been able to prize a word from Sara, not even "mama." Doctors didn't know how that hurt. Smiling now, Rachel tried to coax Sara into her watery lap.

"Sara wants to look for seashells," Pete said.

"There aren't any shells here, only pebbles." Caroline flounced her words like she did her head of silken brown curls. "You find shells at the beach where there's an ocean."

"She's pretending she's at the ocean," answered Pete, ignoring, as he always did, Caroline's precociousness.

Rachel slanted a look at Pete. That he could somehow interpret Sara's silences fascinated her. She had never seen a signal pass between them, yet they shared a secret language. She said by rote what she always said to him, with little conviction or hope. "Sara can speak for herself, Pete."

"Do you think we'll ever go to the beach, Mama? On vacation?" Caroline dipped water with an old tin cup, splashing it on her shoulders. She never put her head under water. "You can't breathe under water. If your head was supposed to go under, you'd have gills like a fish," she had said the first time Pete had tried to get her to explore the bottom of the creek.

Practical cynical Caroline. Rachel knew Caroline was hiding her fears behind a measured wall of solid youthful logic, and there were times when Rachel envied that wall. Except that Caroline sometimes built that wall too high, too thick, keeping even Rachel out.

"Don't be stupid, Caroline," Pete scoffed. "Vacations cost money."

"Don't talk to your sister that way," put in Rachel. "And yes, we will go to the beach . . . someday."

"You promise?"

"No. I just hope," Rachel answered swiftly, avoiding making a promise. Promises could trap. Clive's promises had trapped her, hadn't they?

"Company comin'," announced Pete quietly. They all watched as gray dust furled skyward, marking a vehicle's progress on the one-lane switchback road that led into their yard from the highway.

Standing up, water draining rapidly in thick runnels out of the pockets of her blouse and shorts until the fabric clung to her like a second skin, Rachel ordered, "Up to the porch, all of you. I left towels on the railing."

The car was in the yard, braking to a stop under the mulberry tree before Rachel reached the porch behind the racing youngsters. She recognized the driver as he emerged, unfolding his long rope-muscled body. He adjusted his hat brim with hands that were large and powerful and brutal looking.

A dull ache rose in the back of her throat. She found it impossible to swallow. Sheriff Garrett Stark was a man's man. Everyone in the county came under his mesmerizing spell, his whiskey-and-tobacco drawl, his smooth charm belying a certain roguishness that endowed his lined angular face with an odd sort of appeal. He wore well-cut pressed khakis laundered so often they were like chamois. Rolled-up sleeves exposed tanned muscular arms and the pants pulled taut at the back of his calves. And, of course, he wore the hat. An old brown felt thing that had once belonged to his father and to which Garrett was uncommonly attached. The only thing the hat needed to seem as if it were out of some adventure story was a leopard-skin band. Garrett Stark carried himself in such a manner that you just knew he would have been right at home in any rough-and-tumble, hard-talking movie.

As the villain, Rachel thought uncharitably, knowing Garrett's history. The inhabitants of Lackawanna County, Arkansas, believed they lived in the best county, in the best state, in the best country in the world. They did not change their residence on a whim. If the children, and they meant anyone under forty, wanted to see the world, "let 'em" was the consensus. "But sooner or later," they said, "Lackawanna County reclaims its own." Garrett Stark had been reclaimed.

Big for his age, he had joined the Marines at fifteen and stayed in for twenty years, returning to Arkansas to find his hometown overrun with dope peddlers, gamblers, bootleggers and truants. He was a deputy for two years until he got elected sheriff last year. He had chopped up every still in Lackawanna County, escorted alleged dope peddlers to the county line and closed down the illegal casino in the back room of Nester's Café. He changed flat tires for locals, but gave the business to townsfolk if it was a stranded tourist. He hauled drunks home to be chastised by their angry wives and locked up teens overnight, giving their parents at least one night's sleep in knowing where their children were. He picked up runaways and let them ride on patrol all day or night, depositing them on their doorstep with new purpose at the end of his shift. He took out-of-staters home to his mother with whom he lived. Lackawanna County respected this man with the iron hand, soft voice and light-colored eyes that had a force and a certain mystery. Inviting eyes with a hypnotic gaze that, together with his soft words, had stopped more than one altercation.

He was pointed out as a visible symbol of justice, order and proof of the old-timers' convictions. "Said he'd come back, didn't I?" There were some who looked askance at his appeal, but they were few.

Rachel prided herself on being able to resist Garrett Stark's charm, virility and swagger. But then, she had good cause to resist. He was the reason she was a widow. He was the reason she was suffering so. From the moment they met face-to-face for the first time five months earlier, their hostility had been mutual and instinctive.

In the hot breeze her chestnut hair had begun to dry, and the gleaming sun accentuated the red highlights. It was drawn back from her forehead and held there by a large barrette, and the simple fresh style emphasized the high arches of her cheekbones, flushed now with remembered hurt and anger. She knew her wet clothes clung to her, but there was nothing she could do about it. Nor could she hide that aura of a woman who, having been slender all of her life, cannot, at thirty-two, accustom herself to the voluptuousness that nature bestows on the mature woman. But Rachel faced an enemy, the man who was the direct cause of the disaster that had befallen her, so her spine was straight and her step fluid and smooth as she left the path, waving her children to remain on the safety of the porch, out of earshot. It was the maneuver of a lioness with her cubs, and neither the svelte movement nor the gesture escaped Garrett Stark's keen eyes.

Rachel halted on a small rise of earth, a rostrum from which to address him, though it by no means gave her height over him.

"You're not welcome here, Garrett Stark. Get off my land."

He tipped his hat respectfully, studying her gravely for a moment before he spoke, his gaze including a measure of sexual candor. "Didn't think I would be, but I like to know what's going on with folks in my county."

"*Your* county! What conceit!"

"Just a figure of speech," he replied, unmoved by her outburst. He leaned casually against his car, pulled a cigar from his pocket, peeled the cellophane from it, bit the end off with sharp white teeth, lit it and drew heavily until there was gray ash at the tip. "Heard you and the children had moved back to your old homestead and nobody'd seen you in town. Just thought I'd—"

"What you heard was that our home was repossessed, that I sold everything we had that wasn't nailed down to try and keep it and that I still lost it. That's what you heard. You don't have to pretend to be nice about it. Being nice somehow just doesn't suit you." The tempo of her anger was making her voice quake.

The shifts of Rachel's mood were mirrored in her huge gray-green eyes. It fascinated Garrett to see their color change. It was her eyes that made her whole face what it was. He had never seen another pair of eyes quite like them. It wasn't because they were gray-green or double lashed, but because they looked starry. He wasn't a poet so that was the best he could do to describe them. He speculated that the dewy look hid an impressive intellectual acuity and a wild impulsive nature that could drive a man to his limits. His eyes lingered on her. Her figure was noticeable. Couldn't be anything but noticeable since her dripping clothes were beguilingly delineating the contours of her body. Her breasts were symmetrical and perfectly proportioned, accentuating her small waist, rounded hips and wonderfully shaped legs. She had no fat, her body having been tempered and refined by the physical labor required to "make-do" on the run-down farm over the past several months. The summer sun had burnished her with a flattering tan. She was nubile and alluring and, surprisingly, did not seem aware of it. He couldn't take his eyes off her.

"You're right, that's what I heard. Never knew anyone to call me nice. I like it, though." At last, he dropped his gaze to the cigar he held between thumb and forefinger.

Was it her imagination or had his gaze lingered just a little too long? A surge of anger rose and stuck in Rachel's throat, almost choking her. She watched him draw hard on his cigar, his eyes slitted against the unfurling smoke. "'Nice' is the last thing I'd call you. Maybe you'd like to hear the first?"

"I didn't come out here to pick a fight with you. I guess the reason you haven't been to town is that flat on the wagon. I'll change it for you and be on my way."

"No! I don't want you to do anything for me. I don't want you to be able to assuage your conscience."

A vein began to throb in Garrett's temple, his eyes probing hers in a way that made Rachel's heart pump hard. He had a presence that demanded attention. But not her attention. Never!

Steely controlled anger whipped through Garrett. He lowered the volume of his voice, but not its force. "Still looking at Clive Cameron through rose-colored glasses, aren't you, Rachel? I didn't kill him. He killed himself. The sooner you face that, the sooner you'll be able to get on with your life instead of hibernating out here in the woods. I'll change that tire now."

Rachel clenched and unclenched her fists. "I hate you, Garrett Stark," she uttered softly, so that her voice would not carry to the children. "I hate you to the very depths of my soul."

"Can't say that you're the first," he answered, and waving to the youngsters hanging over the porch railing, he strode around his car to hers and began hauling out the spare tire.

Filled with a seething frustration, Rachel watched him for several seconds, then spun off the mound of earth and stalked to the porch. "All of you, in the house and into dry clothes."

"Maybe I can help him fix the tire," Pete suggested.

Rachel resisted the urge to scream. "No, he doesn't need any help. Get into dry clothes. Now. All of you. Caroline, you help Sara." There was enough rigid authority in her tone that, for once, the children didn't argue.

The house had two rooms if one counted the airy loft, reached by rough-hewn steps built into a side wall, where the children slept. Rachel had painted a section of wood latticework and hung it from a beam to separate Pete's half from the girls'.

The first level of the house held a stove, refrigerator and double sink along one wall. The opposite wall was taken up with a huge stone fireplace in which four-foot sections of trees could be burned. A rump-sprung sofa faced the fireplace. Everyone's favorite spot was the sturdy trestle table on the kitchen side of the room. Far back of the living area beneath the loft was where Rachel had made her bedroom. It was cozy and she had a measure of privacy there. The bathroom had been added on to the house thirty years earlier; it was reached by going out the side door near the sink and onto the porch that wrapped two sides of the house. Rachel went there now to change into dry clothes—

jeans and an old sweatshirt with its sleeves cut out. She brushed her hair and reclamped the barrette. As she emerged onto the side porch, she discovered Garrett striding toward the front.

The screened door had rusted off its hinges, and in the heat the huge wooden door that kept out inquisitive animals at night was latched back against the wall to encourage a lazy summer draft. Rachel confronted Garrett before he could barrel his way across the threshold. He had removed his hat and his lived-in face glowered under a sheaf of jet-black hair that looked as if he had combed it with his fingers. Which he had. Another one of the practiced ways by which he tried to look appealing, thought Rachel. "What is it now?" she asked, barely civil.

"I'm afraid I have bad news. The spare's flat, too."

"Well, then," she replied stiffly, "just forget it and go about your business. There must be some criminals lurking in Lackawanna County that you haven't put the squeeze on yet."

Garrett tried to stare her down while a good half dozen retorts rose to his tongue. He bit down hard on the cigar and talked around it. "I'll take it with me and have it fixed. It'll be a few hours before I can get back, though."

"No! I'll get it fixed myself. I—I'll . . ." Oh, damn! Every little setback was a major catastrophe these days.

"You might need your transportation," he said, smarting with agitation. "One of the kids might break an arm or get snakebit . . . how'd you get them to the doctor? You don't have a phone out here, do you?"

He would pick the fear that worried her most. "You have no right, no right," she whispered, her voice rising, "to lecture me on my responsibilities, Garrett

Stark. If you were worried about me, these children..." She flailed her arm to take in the loft where she knew the children were listening to every word, or trying to. Her voice dropped to reach his ears only. "Why didn't you worry about Clive? Tell me that. Why did you lock him up and walk away, leaving him to . . . to . . . ?" Five months had not dulled the pain. Rachel blinked it back and went on. "I know my responsibilities far better than you!" Oh, how she knew them, wrestled with them, ached with them. To be the only human being responsible for the three tiny lives, depended upon for their every need—food, shelter, clothing, love. If one of them got hurt . . . Or worse, if anything should happen to her . . . The fear lay ragged at the edge of her mind day and night. What of her children then? It didn't bear thinking about. Some of what was running through her mind must have been reflected in her face for Garrett's agitation lessened.

"I'll have the tire fixed and bring it back, Rachel. You'll need the wagon sooner or later."

"I don't want you to—"

His heavy sigh expressed the chafing of a busy man. "How do you propose to stop me? Twist my arm? Break my legs? Shoot me?" He smiled, a nice smile that revealed his large square teeth holding his cigar neatly in place. Rachel hated him for smiling like that, for his knowing light-colored eyes gleaming like stones under water.

"You're caught between a rock and a hard place, Rachel. I'm just trying to soften up one or the other for you."

Not having a choice churned miserably inside her. Pride bade her to run him off her land, but her good sense told her that she needed the tire repaired so she accepted finally with undisguised ill grace. "Go do it, then," she muttered. "Salve your conscience any way you can."

There were some things a man had to go to a woman for, Garrett registered, but a scrap wasn't one of them. He resented Rachel's gall. He was the sheriff. Elected. He was only trying to help. Taking the cigar out of his mouth and leaning toward her, Garrett tapped Rachel on the chest, his voice now as flat and expressionless as leaden air before a storm. "You're a damned stubborn woman, Rachel Cameron. If you didn't have the little ones out here, I wouldn't care if those tires rotted into infinity, or if that piece of banged-up junk spent the rest of its days rusting on its belly."

His fingertip on her chest was not a lingering touch, yet Rachel felt a sudden inexplicable apprehension, an electric surge through her nerves that seemed like a warning. She stepped out of his reach, her eyes flashing with insult. "I knew the first moment I laid eyes on you months ago that you were a mean, hateful, uncaring man. How you've fooled everyone else in this county and got yourself elected sheriff is beyond me. It won't happen again. I'll be the first in line to vote against you in the next election." But all the words she spoke now could not undo the fact that she had once cast her vote for Garrett Stark, right alongside her husband. She shivered. And five months ago, Garrett Stark had betrayed the trust she had placed in him when she had cast that vote.

The air between them was deathly still for a heartbeat, then Garrett jammed the cigar between his teeth, spun on his heel and bounded off the porch.

Leaning weakly against the doorjamb watching him go, Rachel muttered, "Horse's ass."

In his car, stabbing a match to the end of his dead cigar, Garrett growled, "Witch."

2

"WHY DOESN'T SHERIFF STARK carry a gun?" asked Caroline, coming up behind her mother.

"Because he thinks he can charm crooks into Lackawanna County Jail, that's why."

Hearing her mother's tone but knowing it wasn't aimed at her, Caroline's eyes narrowed slightly. "You mean he jinxes them? Is that what he did to Daddy?"

Rachel went very still. This was dangerous ground. "No, and your daddy wasn't—"

"The kids at school said Daddy was a thief. That's why he got arrested."

Rachel found her mouth was suddenly dry. Pete and Caroline had never spoken before of anything that had been said at school. Perhaps the distance of summer vacation, this limbo in which they lived, made it easier for them to talk of things past. Things that must have hurt them terribly after the numbness of shock had worn off. She gazed for a minute out at the mountains before shifting to her daughter. Seeing the young wizened face, sensing the need for truth, she said, "Your father was not a thief. He was accused. There's a difference. Anyone can be accused of something. It was never proved and it never will be."

"Then why was he arrested?"

"Because someone *thought* he was.... Haven't you ever been accused of something that you didn't do?"

"It happens all the time around here," Caroline shot back.

Rachel laughed, relieved that the topic could so easily be changed, but there was an emptiness inside her, a loss, shadowy and unnamed. "Caro, you little stink. Are you conning me?"

The child adopted her most insulted expression, pug nose tilted up, lips pursed, hands on hips. "Once, in the first grade, Amy Williams said I took a dime off her desk, but later she found it on the floor under her seat."

"That's the same situation that your daddy found himself in, Caroline."

"Then why did he . . ."

Why did he die? "I don't know, pumpkin. He took the answer to that with him." Rachel's voice faltered. She made herself glance across to Pete and Sara, both of whom were listening and pretending not to. Children were smart, so smart—too smart sometimes. A sadness surrounded her like the breeze, a sadness that had nothing to do with reason. She felt so lonely, so unsure. "We left the sandwiches at the creek," she said. "The chickens will have got to them by now. Caroline, you and Sara get me a couple of eggplants and some onions from the garden. Pete, did you check the fish trap?"

"I forgot."

"Well, do it now. Fried trout sounds good for supper."

Pete cleared his throat, a sure sign he had something to say. Rachel looked at him expectantly.

"I was worrying how we'd get into town if we had to. It was nice of Sheriff Stark to see to the tire."

Rachel closed her eyes. Always the conciliator was Pete, even when his father had been alive. She wished she had her son's strength, his courage. She heard herself say, as if from some vast distance, "Yes, yes it was."

SITTING ON THE PORCH SWING, activating it now and again with a nudge from her slender bare foot, Rachel watched the moon. Full and yellow, it made hypnotic reflections in the rippling waters of the creek. The night was ripe with summer smells and had that special crystal clarity. It was like being at the bottom of a stream of absolutely clear water. Stars did not twinkle, but hung in the heavens like a thousand trapped suns. Night creatures had not begun to stir or sing; only the sound of a hen stretching her wings, a peculiar fluttering as if a fan were being opened and shut, came to her. The humid July heat had thickened and deepened so that she knew, despite the clear sky, rain was in the offing.

She lit one of her precious cigarettes. It was a nasty habit, and expensive, but she couldn't give it up—not entirely. She limited herself to one in the morning with her coffee, and one at night after the children were in bed. Funny how the smallest thing gave her pleasure now.

Or displeasure. Like Garrett Stark. There were those who called him honest, fair, kindhearted, God-fearing. Rachel knew better. He was notorious, venal, a scoundrel, a rogue, a pervert; he was in league with the devil and he hadn't brought her tire back as he'd said he would. Just to spite her for speaking her mind.

If she closed her eyes, which she would not do, she could call up his face, the smell of his cigar and soap, and the indefinable fragrance of freshly ironed khakis. It made her think about sex. She missed sex. She missed having strong arms around her, missed feeling secure. She hated this feeling of uncertainty and isolation. Love had a way of pushing fear aside. Somehow, with two worrying, burdens were lessened, disappointments made easier, laughter more spontaneous. She could not remember the last time she had truly laughed.

She caught her toe on a loose plank and cursed mildly, then folded one knee across the other so that she could check her toe for splinters. She behaved childishly now when she got hurt, or when anything happened to thwart her. Once, when a pot of rice had boiled over, she found herself crying. That was what widowhood did to a woman—she indulged in bouts of wild self-pity too often. Dying was inhumane for those who were left behind. Any kind of dying was, but Clive Cameron's was worst of all. It heaped guilt upon those who had to live.

Crickets began their night song, a fish leaped in the creek, sending out ripples of moon-gold light. Rachel stubbed out her cigarette and walked to the edge of the porch to stare at the creek. The sheriff had gotten an eyeful when she had climbed that incline today. There was enough woman in her, enough ego, enough longing to hope that he was suffering for it.

THE RAIN BEAT a soothing tattoo on the roof. Rachel snuggled deeper beneath the coverlet, deeper into the lovely dream she was having. A dream of warm sensations and safety. The tattoo became more insistent, not like rain at all. Instinct cut through her sleep-drugged body and she sat up. The stubborn rapping was at the front door. She glanced out the window. Weak gray light, past dawn. It was Garrett Stark. She knew it with a dull certainty. It was like him to arrive high and mighty when decent folk were still abed. She drew on her robe, fumbling with the sash as she made her way to the door.

Garrett Stark did not look lordly. The lines of his face had deepened, his eyes were bloodshot and rain dripped steadily from the brim of his hat. The cigar clamped between his teeth drooped. In the damp his khakis had lost their snap. Still, he had an air of superb masculine virility. Rachel ran her fingers through her chestnut hair, unconsciously arranging it into attractive dishabille while her heart and head pounded in different rhythms.

"Do you know what time it is?" she asked in high dudgeon. Her gray-green eyes flickered, smoldering with outrage at him and at her own voice, which was alluring and throaty with leftover sleep.

Garrett felt the confusion that tensed her body as if it were his own. He could smell faintly the enticing perfume of her hair. "Early. A diesel overturned on the highway, spewing ammonia. We had to work all night diverting traffic. I didn't want to go off duty without dropping the tire by." He took off his hat, shaking water from it; a lock of damp black hair fell boyishly over his brow. "But I'll have to wait until the rain lets up before I change it."

"Keep your voice down or you'll wake the children, and I don't want you to wait—"

"Am, though." He spoke quietly, didn't move, not a muscle, except his eyes, and they swept over her with such intensity, Rachel seemed to feel their caress.

She pretended not to notice until their eyes met and held, while something uncommon, illogical, unbidden went between them. Her body began to shake. A chill skittered the length of her spine, growing warmer every downward inch it traveled until there was an unmistakable sensuous heat pervading the slopes and hollows of her body; gaining momentum, it gathered and collected in her most secret places. Speechless, she waited for the throbbing sensation to vanish. But the warmth blazed with the tenacity of a fire begun in well-seasoned wood. She cloaked it with anger and rasped in a small husky voice, "Then wait it out on the porch on the swing, damn you."

His bold gaze shifted. "There's a gully washer of a leak over that swing."

"And you might melt," she retorted with silvery sweetness, closing the door in his face, catching herself just in time to keep from slamming it, but leaning against it weakly once the latch clicked with finality.

Shaken himself, Garrett placed a hand on the jamb, staring at the closed door with a combination of stupefaction and vehemence. He had felt the extraordinary current that had swept through them. He hadn't planned it, hadn't anticipated it, sure as hell didn't want it. His imagination, that's all it was. He was seeing and feeling strange things because he was suffering from exhaustion. Like getting a bump on the head and suffering double vision. Same thing. He didn't take to women like Rachel Cameron—sharp-tongued, steely, boneheaded. It put a man off from noticing her flashing eyes, the provocative curve of her mouth, her full breasts and shapely legs. Suddenly, Garrett felt a peculiar stirring deep within himself. Airylike, burning. The chili he ate at Nester's Café last night. That was it. He tossed his soggy cigar into the yard and began unwrapping another. He looked down at his hands in amazement: they were shaking.

Ignoring the tautness of her nerves, Rachel expelled a tumultuous breath as she went upstairs to the loft. The children were still solidly asleep. A wonderfully cool, damp breeze came in the dormer windows. She rearranged their sheets, making sure Pete's feet were uncovered. Let a scrap of blanket touch them, winter or summer, and he would be awake in a flash. She meant to be rid of Garrett Stark before anyone awakened with innocent inquisitive questions.

Downstairs, she gathered up her jeans and shirt, slipping—sneaking—out the door onto the side porch. She slid around the old four-legged washing machine that she had hated with a passion as a teenager; now she prayed silently that its hand-cranked wringer would never wear out. In the bathroom she brushed her teeth and dressed. Deliberately, she did not apply cosmetics, but cold water splashed on her face put color in her tanned cheeks and, as was her wont, she pinned her hair atop her head against the damp. Her mirror image answered Pete's question: was she still pretty? She didn't mean to be, not this morning, especially not for Garrett Stark.

When she tiptoed into the house, she found him leaning back in a chair at the trestle table, his arms folded contentedly across his chest, smoke spiraling ceilingward. She halted just inside the threshold. "You—! Coming into my house this way is breaking and entering," she hissed. "I did *not* ask you in. Get out!"

"Keep your voice down or you'll wake the kids."

She whispered, "I will not allow you to heap insult upon injury." Her chin came up, drawing taut the flesh on her neck so that pulsebeats in its hollows were visible. Her eyes widened, huge and liquid, shadowy with frustration. "You think you can bully me because I'm a woman. Well, you can't." Her gaze darted around the room, lighting on the broom within reach. She grabbed it and began swinging.

"For crying out loud—" Garrett uttered hoarsely, catching the straw in midswing. "I was about to fall asleep standing up. I knocked . . . you didn't answer. I went around to the side door and heard you in the bathroom. So I came in and got a pot of coffee going. Otherwise I'd have to sit in my car, and if I did that and closed my eyes, the walls of Jericho crashing down wouldn't wake me. I pulled a double shift because one of my deputies had to go down to Hot Springs to testify in a trial."

"You think that gives you the right to just walk into my house like you own it?"

A sigh welled up; he forced it back. "Maybe not. But a little courtesy on your part would go a long way. Don't you have any feelings for a fellow human being?"

"Not for you, I don't." Her bearing was positively glacial.

"Turn loose your end of the broom," he urged, watching her through a thin slit of dark lashes.

Knowing she couldn't match his strength, Rachel let the broom fall. His powerful hand loosened its grip, eating up the handle. He placed it beside his chair.

Though he wasn't letting it show, Garrett was fuming inside. Rachel Cameron's bravery was on the wrong side of imprudence. Attacking him with a broom! If that ever got around the county—the thought wasn't to be borne. He changed tactics. He had to. God wasn't really a man or He wouldn't keep on creating original Eves. "I could arrest you right now for assaulting a peace officer," he said.

"I wouldn't put it past you. But then, I'd charge you with trespassing." It was taking a tremendous effort for

Rachel to calm herself; the rapid rise and fall of her breasts beneath the thin cotton shirt revealed the struggle.

Hell and damnation! Garrett cursed silently. He could feel his groin tightening. The woman was a regular sylph, going around without underwear like she did. He puffed hard on the cigar. "I could arrest you first. Of course, I'd release you on your own recognizance, seeing as you're a mother and all—if I could just have a couple o' cups of coffee. It's perked now."

"I'm not afraid of you, or your threats," Rachel told him archly, glowering. But she was. She was actually, *actually*, thinking of him as a man and had been since their eyes had locked. Those feelings, those longings that had erupted had been buried so deeply in her feminine core, so layered with pain and grief and guilt, that she had never expected them to surface again. Dazed with discovery, she strode to the stove, poured coffee, then sat across from him. "I won't be bullied," she continued. "Everyone already knows how you prey on the innocent, making up charges so you'll look good to the county commissioners." She took a sip of coffee and felt the steaming brew burn all the way down to her stomach. "Since you've made yourself so at home in *my* house, you can get your own coffee."

"You don't give an inch, do you? If you're ever lookin' for work, you ought to try Nester's. They make it a habit to hire women like you, just to give folks like me indigestion."

Her smile was mocking. "You're so deserving, Sheriff."

He took a step away from the table, then turned back, his glance scornful, and got the broom, setting it outside. "Wouldn't want to put temptation in front of you now that we're getting along so well."

The rain continued to fall, seeming not to slacken at all. The children slept on. Rachel and Garrett sat across from each other. Silent. Pretending the other did not exist. By the time Rachel had smoked three of her precious cigarettes, Garrett had begun to nod.

"Don't you dare go to sleep. Don't you dare!"

He jerked his head up. "Maybe I should have a bite to eat, get my metabolism going. Never could sleep on a full stomach."

"Why don't you just leave? I can change that tire, I'm not helpless. Pete will help me."

"The weather's bound to let up soon."

"Suppose it doesn't?"

He was silent for so long, Rachel thought she might have to prod him. "I hate to tell you this, but I'm too sleepy to drive home."

A surge of panic rose and stuck in Rachel's throat, almost choking her.

"Mornin', Mama."

Rachel's and Garrett's heads swiveled as if caught flagrante delicto. Pete and Caroline were draped over the loft banister, arms dangling. Sara, too short for such catlike dexterity, was sitting, her stubby legs thrust through the openings, sucking her thumb and holding a doll.

Garrett said, "Hi, kids."

Rachel said, "Make your beds and get dressed. Breakfast in fifteen minutes." She had no choice but to put a plate of bacon and eggs and blueberry muffins in front of Garrett lest the children sense that there was a strain between them, or misconstrue her lack of courtesy.

"You been here all night?" Pete asked the sheriff.

Garrett cleared his mouth of muffin. "Worked all night," he said after a sip of coffee. "Just stopped by to change that tire."

"Did you?"

"Not yet. Will, though, soon as the rain stops."

"That's good. Mama and I could maybe do it, but once when I was helping Daddy change a flat, the car slipped off the jack."

"Your eyes are bloodshot," said Caroline to Garrett.

"Caroline!" remonstrated her mother.

"Well, they are, Mama. And you said to always tell the truth."

Rachel was torn between chastising her daughter and avoiding further embarrassment. She had been a mother too long to let it slide. "I didn't necessarily mean to someone's face. That kind of truth is rude."

"But, you said, even if it hurts . . ."

Rachel touched her fingertips to her temples. It was impossible to win against this child's simple logic. She caught Garrett's eye. There was a mocking tilt at one corner of his mouth. He was enjoying her discomfort.

"Like mother, like daughter," he mouthed silently, and then Sara caught his attention. Waiflike, she fed herself a forkful of eggs, then offered eggs to the doll she was holding in her lap. Garrett had not spent much time around children, but he sensed at once that there was something special about her. Suddenly, he imagined how difficult it would be—was—for all of them not to have their father around, not to ever see him again. Garrett hated death. It was cruel, for it waited and hid behind every corner and snatched up man, woman or child without the slightest warning. At sixteen, he had seen his first dead man, in Asia. He would never forget it, never forget the man's brutally contorted body.

Clive Cameron had liked easy money and had gone after it. Garrett, in the line of duty, had stalked the man and caught him at it. Damn! He wished he had known that Cameron was weak, that he had a sickness. He wished he had not walked away from the jail cell that night so that Clive Cameron could turn his children into orphans, or almost orphans. For Clive Cameron had embraced his own death, he had destroyed himself. It could not be blamed on a cruel god. Yet there was no halfway about Rachel. She was a widow. The thought trailed. Single. Available.

Dishes rattled. Startled, Garrett looked blankly around him. The children had been sent to wash up, their mother was clearing the table. The rain was drumming steadily on the roof. Rachel's tone was at the cutting edge of anger. "If you have to snooze, go do it on the sofa. Sleeping at the table is bad manners. And don't you ever, ever come here acting like a sleep-walker again. You—you put me on the spot in front of the kids."

He was too tired to form much of a protest. "I wasn't thinking," he mumbled, stumbling wearily to the sofa.

"That seems to be a failing of yours."

Garrett didn't hear. Feet hanging past the end of the sofa, his elbow crooked over his eyes, he was in an-other world, leaving Rachel awash with fractiousness at having to keep her children quiet and occupied while the man she hated most in the world got his beauty sleep.

There was another emotion within her besides hate as she stared at the dark shadows under Garrett's closed eyes and the deep lines in his forehead. She felt the urge to touch him, to smooth out the lines, and fought with herself until it was driven from her mind. It was one more thing to hate him for—arousing this need in her. She had forgotten what it was like to long for a man, to ache for release as if it were salvation. She would be days putting it down again.

3

GARRETT TURNED OVER and rolled off the sofa, hitting his funny bone and yelping groggily in pain. He heard a giggle and opened his eyes, focusing on its source. Caroline sat on the rock hearth, her arm draped about her younger sister. Both girls were viewing him as they would some exotic animal in a zoo. Early afternoon sunlight streamed through the open window bringing with it the sharp odor of wet pine and rain-washed air.

"You sleep with your mouth open," observed Caroline.

Bleary-eyed, Garrett tried to stare her down and couldn't. "How old are you?"

Caroline sniffed. "Seven, going on eight."

"If you don't learn to use a little guile, you're going to grow up to be an old maid."

"I never heard of 'guile.'" Her tone implied that since she hadn't, it probably didn't exist.

"Where's your mother?"

"On the porch, washing clothes."

He pulled himself to his feet, rubbing his elbow. His beard stubble was thick and every muscle in his body ached from sleeping cramped on the lumpy sofa. When he came out of a long stretch and a wide yawn, Rachel was standing before him.

"Rain's stopped. You can change that tire now, if you're still insisting."

"Good afternoon to you, too."

"Good will be when I've seen your back."

"Could you spare a cup of coffee to wake me up?"

While her sensitive face creased in hesitant lines, the set of her chin became rigid. *Give this man an inch,* she thought, *and he takes a mile.* "You start on the car. I'll bring it to you when it's hot."

He took in her stance, gaze narrowed through thick lashes, lower lip trembling just enough to give her away, arms folded protectively across her breasts. A smile warred with his irritation. "You remind me of a captain I once knew when I was in the Marines, a book man to the bone. One of his own men shot him in . . ." Remembering his audience, Garrett stopped himself just in time. "Where's that boy of yours? He wanted to help."

"Right here!" Pete answered from the porch.

"Don't track mud," cautioned Rachel, glad of the interruption that turned away the sheriff's probing eyes.

"Let's get on with it, then," said Garrett, giving Rachel one last calculating glance. He was whistling a nameless tune by the time he reached the threshold.

Watching him place his hand on the back of Pete's neck as he joined her son, Rachel felt a sense of waste, of unfinished business. She dropped her arms to her sides and went to make fresh coffee.

A light sweat began to bead her forehead. She could no longer follow her own thoughts. Her body wouldn't let her. She could feel sensations surging up, filling her, enveloping her, writhing their way beneath the chaste celibate sheath in which she had cloaked her erotic emotions. Garrett Stark had looked at her as if she were a desirable woman. He had looked hard, and kept on looking so that now a phantom of recalled sensual pleasure shot through her. It wasn't fair! She had been doing so well. How could she be drawn so to . . . to the very man she blamed for her widowhood? It was beyond comprehension.

He was doing it on purpose. That was it. Of course. She knew his reputation. He'd take on any woman over eighteen and under forty. She'd heard that in Hickory Grove. Women fawned over him. Well, he had another think coming if he thought Rachel Cameron— mother, widow, soon-to-be teacher—would fall all over him. She was just getting her emotions, her life into some kind of order. No one was going to *un*order it.

By the time the coffee was perked and poured into a mug, her hand was steady and her face composed. Turmoil did not show through. She was proud of that, and the proudness gave her an edge when she joined Garrett beneath the dripping mulberry tree.

His shirt was as soaked as if he'd spent ten minutes in the rain. She looked away from his bulging biceps as he tightened the lugs on the wheel. Pete was sitting in the patrol car listening to the police-band radio. "Here's your coffee," she said.

He tossed the lug wrench aside and stood up. "Thanks."

"You're welcome."

"Am I?"

"It just slipped out. Habit."

"Figures." He leaned on the fender, sipping from the cup. Rachel felt awkward just standing there, not talking.

"Did you tell Pete he could sit in your car?"

Garrett nodded.

"Any guns in there?"

He gave her a withering look. "Shotgun's locked in the trunk. I'm not that shortsighted."

"You were once."

He stiffened and the hand holding the cup tightened as if to crush it. "I'm going to tell you this once, and only once, so listen good." His voice had dropped to a guttural whisper. "Clive Cameron liked easy money. He cruised the highways and back roads for stalled and abandoned cars, and not just in my county. He took batteries, tape decks, tires, suitcases—and sold them across the county line. I caught him driving away from one in this very junk heap of yours." He tapped the roof with his fist, softly, controlled. "He had a pair of speakers he'd torn out of the back seat."

The man seemed so certain, so sure of himself, Rachel's hackles rose. Determination and loyalty welled up. "I don't believe you. You're just maligning the dead." Somewhere nearby a cricket sounded, its chorus a soft salute to her words.

"It doesn't matter," he said, tight-lipped. Somehow, though, it did matter. This discovery brought with it a measure of clarity. He knew he could convince her. He cursed the civilized instinct that stopped him. The stricken look on her face touched him, made him want to reach out to her, protect her. Surprised at his own reaction, he shook his head as if to clear it of muddled thoughts. He put the cup on the roof of the station wagon, gathered up the old tire, the jack, the lug wrench, tossing them into the back of the wagon, then got behind the wheel.

"Wait! What're you doing?"

His light-colored eyes were cold, a striking contrast to the dark thick beard stubble on his square jaw. "I'm going to move it back a length. It's kind of muddy here.

Don't want you stuck." It was a tone of voice usually reserved for making a threat.

Rachel understood. He didn't want to be rescuing her at every turn or mishap. "I can do it."

His answer was to turn the key in the ignition. The motor didn't start. He tried again. Nothing. He closed his eyes and dropped his head on folded arms on the steering wheel and expelled a muffled groan.

"What's—what's the matter?"

"Battery's dead."

"Oh, no."

"Oh, yes," he mimicked, his sarcasm as heavy as lead.

The knot in Rachel's stomach was reminiscent of all the times she had failed to cope with the unexpected over the past months. The palms of her hands grew moist. "Maybe it's something else?"

"It probably is," Garrett equivocated morosely. "But the first thing is a dead battery, and I don't have my cables in the car." He didn't know whether he wanted to laugh or cry. "I'll send someone out from Deke's Station to charge it up for you."

"No!" Her voice was too sharp and Rachel regretted it immediately. Color suffused her face.

Garrett's voice went gritty. "What the hell do you mean, 'no'?"

"No, I...we...can't afford Deke's. Way out here like this he'd charge..." Her voice trailed off, and she looked away.

"Is everything okay, Mama?" asked Pete in a hushed voice. He came around the rear of the station wagon, his expression tense, eyes troubled.

"Everything's fine—"

"Just a slight difference of opinion, son," added Garrett, emerging from the car, aware that the boy's eyes tracked his every move. It wasn't the first time Pete had sidled up to his mother like that, Garrett thought. Protective. The child's quick response to his mother's sharp tone of dismay gave Garrett an inkling of what Rachel's marriage had been like. The kind of relationship that was kept behind closed doors and pulled shades, but could never be hidden from children with their uncluttered instincts.

"I'll be around with some jumper cables," he said to Rachel.

"Don't make a special trip." She spoke with icy finality.

"Wouldn't think of it." He nodded to Pete. "Take care of your mother, son."

"Yessir, I will."

Garrett glanced once in his rearview mirror before turning into the first switchback on the narrow lane. Rachel was standing beneath the drooping branches of the mulberry tree, one hand on the bony shoulder of the boy, staring after him. She looked so frail, so defenseless. That was one woman who needed a keeper, he thought. But it wasn't going to be him. No way. A woman and marriage could rob a man of his illusions quicker than you could say "Jack Spratt."

Garrett liked his dreams of a perfect wife. She would adore him, never complaining about his cigar. And perfect children. All in his image. A tidy house. Built to his specifications. Maybe he was a closet romantic, but he wasn't above a little dalliance now and again. A man was a man, after all. Just until he got married. But thirty-eight was too young to give up the good life.

The look in Rachel's wide gray-green eyes floated above his thoughts and kept imprinting itself on his brain. The image shuttled back and forth, as if seeking a way out. A fierce feeling of protectiveness surged through him. He felt a fluttering in his gut. By damn! He was going to stop by Nester's on the way home. Old Charlie might have got around to poisoning the whole county by now.

An hour later, Rachel realized she had not paid Garrett for having the tire repaired. She made a note in her budget, hesitating over the amount. Three dollars? Six? Suddenly, she felt as if a steel band were closing about her skull and she fought back the sobs that threatened to burst forth. She could do it. She was good at budgeting, good at scattering pennies where they'd do the most good. She had done it all her married life. It was just fearsome having to go it alone. Garrett's words crept into her thoughts. Clive, a thief! Caught red-handed. She didn't believe it. Clive had stretched out his unemployment checks doing day labor on surrounding farms. That's why he was on those out-of-the-way county roads. Garrett was just trying to cover himself because Clive had died in his jail. The question "why" rose in her mind for the thousandth time. As always, she had no answer.

"Mama, are you going to cook dinner?"

Rachel swung back to the present. "I sure am, Pete. What do you say to vegetable soup and hot corn bread?"

"I wish we had a television."

"To eat?" teased Rachel.

"To watch like we used to."

"We have a radio."

"Music, news and weather reports," he said glumly.

"Nothing wrong with a bit of cheerful music. Suppose we roll back the carpet after dinner and dance."

"We don't have a carpet," piped up Caroline.

"Dance. Yuck! I'd rather skin tomatoes," announced Pete.

"Then Sara and I will perform for you, won't we, pet?" She picked up the child and, delighted with Sara's squeals of laughter, twirled about the room.

"Sometimes you act crazy, Mama." Caroline sounded disapproving.

"Sometimes I am crazy," said Rachel, depositing Sara on the loft steps. She dropped a kiss atop Caroline's head as Caroline went sashaying up the steps past Sara.

"Sheriff Stark has a neat radio," said Pete. "You can hear all the truckers talking. He has a Kojak light, too, on the seat. When he chases somebody he just slaps it on the roof and turns on the siren. He said I can ride with him on patrol sometime. I might be a sheriff when I grow up."

Rachel opened her mouth to protest, then closed it. Pete was only nine. There would be a dozen different jobs that appealed to him before he grew up. He needed a man in his life to look up to, to admire, to emulate. She couldn't let it be Garrett Stark. For the space of a heartbeat she felt a hatred for her dead husband. How could a man father a son and not wish to see him grow, see him become a man in his own image? Another question to which there was no answer. Rachel began to peel potatoes.

4

RACHEL GOT UP with the first cackling of the hens. If Garrett thought to catch her in bed this morning, he had another think coming. She'd be up and waiting for him. Waiting. Not hoping. She couldn't stand him. She had had a miserable restless night. His fault, for stirring emotions out of ashes. Alone in her bed, facing the emptiness of the night and a lifetime more of them just as empty, his face and the manly smell of him had haunted her. She had dreamed of bare flesh against bare flesh, hungry lips, passionate embraces.

Awake, she forced herself away from the remnants of the dream, telling herself that she had good years yet to live—for her children, with her children. That was enough. She'd make it enough. She didn't need a man. She didn't need sex. A swell of anger took hold and she nursed it, rolling it back and forth, recalling all the nasty comments she'd heard about Garrett Stark. She made up a future for herself. She saw herself being gay, laughing, cooking, sewing, becoming a grand-mother—above reproach, above compromise. Celibate. Rachel moved off the bed, rife with a painful yearning in her chest.

Barefoot, dressed in white shorts and a sleeveless blouse, she took her coffee to the front porch. The early morning had a wonderful lush dewy coolness that the summer sun would burn away by ten o'clock.

Rachel couldn't sit still. She brought the ironing board onto the porch, connected an extension cord to the iron, sprinkled water on clothes. Work was an ally, a hidden strength. And because she couldn't help it, now and again she looked up from the ironing, glancing expectantly at the road.

She ran out of coat hangers and when she returned to the porch with a handful, Garrett Stark was parking his car next to hers. She only had a minute to plan how to act, what to say. Fluent in her mind, yet silent of speech, she looked at him as if he were a stranger, soon to be introduced. As he approached she studied his khaki-clad body, the fluid way he moved, and found it good.

"You look domestic," he said, reaching the stoop. His light-colored eyes were penetrating, assessing, invincible. On the surface Rachel found him repellent, insolent in his stance—feet apart, hands on hips, mouth sardonic. Yet she was drawn to him, enjoying the manner in which he stared at her, taking her in. She fought the urge to preen, to act the coquette.

"I am domestic. What did you expect?"

He moved to the swing, sprawling his arms out along its back, stretching his long legs forward and crossing them at the ankles. Rachel stood behind the ironing board, facing him, then took up the iron again. "Just make yourself at home," she said scathingly.

"Kids aren't up yet?"

"No."

"Coffee ready?"

"I drank it all."

"Oh, now . . ."

"Is that what you do all day? Sponge off helpless women?"

"You're helpless?" His words seemed to have no feeling attached to them. In a flash of clarity Rachel understood he was trying to be as casual as she.

She gave an inch. "There might be a cup or so left in the pot. I'll go warm it up." She refilled her own cup, too, setting it at the end of the ironing board. When she handed Garrett his cup he accepted it gingerly, careful not to touch her fingers, so that Rachel almost dropped it during the passing.

"Oh!" She blanched, her eyes flying to meet his, and whatever Garrett expected to prevent in not touching now seemed to spring palpably between them.

"Damn! Did it spill? Are you burned?"

"I'm fine."

She wasn't. She was confused. She hurried to the ironing board, putting it between them. A barrier, as if safety lay in the scorched slick board cover. She tried to will away the eagerness and excitement that was beginning to infuse her mind and body. She felt words rushing to her throat, but she couldn't let them out. She had been too long among the children with no adults to talk to. But she knew exactly where her loyalties lay, and they weren't with Garrett Stark. The minute he had the car going she would take the children and go into Hickory Grove. Even if all they did was walk up and down Main Street and speak to passersby.

"Rachel..." His voice was soft, filled with a substance she refused to name. She made herself focus on him.

"What?"

"You've ironed that shirt twice and inside out."

"Fix the battery and leave, Garrett—please."

"Revving it up will make noise, maybe wake the kids."

"It's time for them to get up anyway." She needed, wanted desperately, the defense of their presence.

"I told the boy he could ride with me today."

"You shouldn't have. You should've asked me first."

Garrett unwrapped a cigar and began searching his pockets for a match. "He asked me. Said he'd been up to his neck in women all summer."

Despite the emotions warring within her, Rachel smiled. "Pete doesn't talk like that. 'Up to his neck in women.' Phooey!"

"I don't mind if he goes. I'll just keep him a few hours."

"Why? Why would you want to?"

Garrett suddenly leaned forward, his eyes glistening, his gaze measuring. "Empathy."

Rachel was stunned. "With me?"

"With the boy. I live with my mother, too."

It was true, but Rachel had trouble seeing Garrett going home to his mama every night. There had to be something wrong with a man Garrett's age who still kept house with his mother. Of course, all the old biddies in Lackawanna County thought it was wonderful of the sheriff to be so kind and thoughtful of Mrs. Stark. Rachel had a notion they were blind to his faults.

"It's not the same," she said with a sniff.

"Mothers are."

The sky was thick with gold, the sun beginning to create heat, loosening the smell of resin from pine sap. Rachel unplugged the iron, took her cup and sat on the stoop with her back to Garrett. She couldn't keep looking at him.

"How many times have you been into town since you moved out here, Rachel? Twice? Three times? You can't hole up out here as if the rest of the world doesn't exist. It's not healthy."

She steeled herself to turn and glare at him. "The way I live, the way I raise my children is none of your concern. We like it here. It's . . . it's peaceful." Her voice dropped. "You let their father die, Garrett. You can't take his place. I won't let you."

He shook his head, muttering an epithet. "I did not let Clive die. Why don't you face facts? And I walk in my own shoes. It's something you ought to keep in mind." He was galled at Rachel's effrontery, comparing him to a weak sister like Clive Cameron, a dead man at that. He wasn't a man to sulk, but he felt like doing it anyway. "Thanks for the coffee." He stalked past her, trailing smoke, and Rachel got a whiff of soap, shaving lotion, tobacco—a heady mixture of maleness that made her stomach tighten. She watched him lift the hoods of both vehicles, then attach the jumper cables. The racing of the motors woke the children, and Rachel went in to them.

"Hey! Sheriff Stark's back," Pete called from the loft. "Why didn't you wake me, Mom? I can ride with him today, can't I? Can't I?"

"I don't think so . . ."

"But we might catch a crook or at least a speeder."

"You might get hurt."

"No, I wouldn't."

"You have your pig and chickens to feed and water."

"Aw, Mom . . ." The pleading in his voice matched the disappointment on his face.

"We'll all go in to Hickory Grove later."

"It's not the same."

Nothing is ever the same, Rachel thought as she put butter-fried toast and eggs on the table. "Eat your breakfast."

Garrett's frame filled the doorway. "Your wagon's running. You need to leave the motor on for twenty minutes or so, let the battery get charged up good."

Rachel faced him. "Thank you and goodbye."

"You're welcome." He nodded at the children, speaking to Pete. "You about ready to go, sport? Got a lot of territory to cover today."

Rachel flew across the room, grabbing Garrett by the arm, dragging him onto the porch. "Stop it!" she hissed. "I told you. He can't go. You're just making it hard on him, and me."

Garrett took her wrists in his huge hands. "Don't get so close, Rachel. I haven't had a woman in a while. You're getting under my skin."

She jerked loose, taking a step back, forcing fury while she rubbed her wrists, trying to erase the imprint of his fingers. "Oh? You're going to add rape to your long list of sordid accomplishments? I want you off my land. I want you out of my life, out of my children's lives. You're not good for them. You're a . . . a reminder."

His voice went soft and grainy. "Rape? You think I'm a man who has to resort to violence to get a woman?" The softness went. "You're one ripe plum for picking, Rachel, only you're hanging on the tree and can't see it for yourself. I know the signs, so lay off that kind of talk. As for being a reminder, you mean I remind you of what you're missing, don't you? Maybe remind you of what you've never had? You want everyone to look on you as a martyr, right? You're too full of yourself, Rachel. And you're taking it out on the kids."

"That's not true! You just think every woman in the county should grovel at your feet. You think we ought to have a high regard for every little crumb of kindness you spill. Well, I don't! I wish you'd never..." There was a sudden quiet in the kitchen. Rachel glanced back through the door, seeing the children's expressions of alarm. "Now look what you've done."

"Me?" Garrett waved his cigar, spread his hands. "You're the one bellowing like a drill sergeant. Look, let the boy ride with me for a couple of hours. I'll take care of him. Bring him back in one piece. I promise."

"What are your promises worth, Garrett?"

"That's something you'll have to discover for yourself, isn't it?"

"Did you talk her into it, Sheriff?" Pete asked, sounding full of innocent hope as he sidled up next to his mother.

Rachel took a deep breath and turned away. She was being forced into being the good guy. She wasn't ready yet to relinquish melancholy, anger, spite. But she felt herself giving in to Garrett, hating herself because the strength of purpose she so depended upon had deserted her. She snatched freshly ironed shorts and a shirt off the ironing board and thrust them at Pete.

"All right. Just this once. Go change."

"Yippee!"

"Happy now?" Rachel spat at Garrett. "Does it make you feel good, your little deed for the day?"

"I'm beginning to see now why Clive took the way out he did."

The sharp taunt hit home. He heard Rachel gasp, heard her sharp sucking breath of surprise, and he wanted suddenly to unsay the words.

The tendons at the back of her neck pulled taut. "That's low," she cried, covering a face drained of color with her hands.

Garrett squirmed inwardly, hating himself for the slip of his tongue, wanting to comfort her, wanting to apologize. "Wait a minute. I didn't mean it like it sounded. You just made me mad. Hell, you're not going to cry, are you?"

"Not in front of you," she snapped. "I wouldn't give you that pleasure." She gathered her resources. "How much do I owe you for the tire and charging the battery?"

Pete came bounding out of the house followed by Caroline and Sara. "I'm ready. See you guys."

"Did you brush your teeth?"

"Brushed everything!" he said, making his escape to the patrol car.

Garrett stepped off the porch and turned back to Rachel. Some color had returned to her cheeks. He took the cigar out of his mouth. "About the tire, Rachel— not 'how much.' Think 'what.'"

Female instinct read the meaning of his words. "Never!" she uttered gutturally at his retreating back. "You think you can insult me in one breath and . . . and . . . in the next! You're warped, Garrett. Warped!" She thought for an instant he would turn, reply, but he lifted his hand to the brim of his hat in a salute, as good as him getting the final word. She wanted to order her son out of the car, but then Garrett would accuse her of using Pete as a weapon. He wouldn't let the opportunity pass. Her hands curling into fists, she watched Garrett help Pete buckle the seat belt and, as the car pulled away, took in his casual wave, his knowing smile.

"This is great," Caroline said. "For once, we're rid of bossy mouth. I hope Sheriff Stark keeps Pete all day. Can I feed the pig, Mama?"

Rachel pulled her mind away from Garrett and gave herself over to what she did best: mothering. "Yes, you can feed the pig. Sara, you can help me make beds."

Would to God, Rachel thought as she moved indoors, that she could make her life all nice and neat like she did the house. Wash away pain, iron out anger, sweep out the debris of hurt and shame and lies. She didn't want to think about Garrett and the influence he might have on Pete. She didn't want to think about Garrett and the influence he was having on herself. Shaking off a bothersome emptiness, she replayed his every word in her mind, his every gesture, suffering hurt at his remark about Clive, suffering too the sudden excitement in her secret places each time she recalled the payment he expected to extract from her. She vowed he'd take cold cash or nothing! Resolute with self-denial, she made the house sparkle. When there wasn't a dust mote left to chase, she took the girls outside to work in the garden and rake the chicken coop and, when she remembered, raced around the house to turn off the motor of the car.

Too late. It had run until it was out of gas. She kept trying to start it, willing it to start. The engine sputtered faintly, then didn't sputter at all.

She sat behind the wheel telling herself that mothers were only supposed to have sufficient power to ward off all evils and the more vicious whims of fate; to provide three meals a day at which creamed spinach, oatmeal and liver were never served; to join the PTA and field scouts; and never to suffer hangnails. Remembering to shut off idling cars was not on the list. Rachel folded her arms on the steering wheel and cried.

"BOY! I LIKE THIS PATROLLING." Pete twisted around in his seat and waved at his friend standing by the riverbank. "Thanks for stopping to let me talk to Billy. I hadn't seen him since school let out. We used to come down here and fish together all the time. Never caught nothin', though. Imagine he was impressed seeing me with you."

Garrett laughed. "I wish everybody thought that."

"You mean my mom?"

"I—no. No, I don't think I mean your mom," replied Garrett, taken aback. "Your mother and I just have a little misunderstanding. But we'll work it out."

"Mom's scared sometimes. She tries not to show it."

"Well, I guess we're all that way now and again."

"You get scared?" Pete's eyes narrowed with disbelief.

"Sure do." He handed Pete a cigar. "Peel that for me, will you?"

"I like riding with you, Sheriff. I like you. Personally, I mean." As always when he came close to blundering, he rushed on to get it finished. "I liked my daddy, too," he added with quick loyalty. "I miss him."

"Dying is hard on everybody."

"I guess it is," said Pete with a weighted sigh. They drove a mile or two in companionable silence. Then Pete began to squirm and fidget.

"If you have something on your mind, son, spit it out."

"He was a thief, wasn't he, like the kids in school said?"

Making a show of biting the end off the cigar and getting it lit, Garrett vied for time to compose an answer, wishing wholeheartedly that he had not opened up that can of worms. A lonely man could get himself into a heap of trouble, he thought, just by taking a young kid out on patrol with him. If he said he was lonely to any one of his contemporaries they would scoff at him in astonishment. He hoped the charm he oozed was real, and he took in stride the snide suggestions that he ought to bottle it. But charisma covered up a lot, including the true state of his soul. He was searching that soul right now for an answer that would satisfy the boy, but he didn't want to lie. It made him feel strange that he wanted Pete's respect. "I thought that your dad was up to something he shouldn't have been. It was just my opinion, though." *With reason*, he thought. "I never proved it."

"That's what Mom says."

"Your mother is one smart woman." He exhaled relief.

"Are you married, Sheriff?"

Garrett choked and sputtered until his eyes watered. He wasn't ready for that much respect. "No..." And for good measure, he added, "And I'm not looking to be."

"My mom's not married, either," said Pete, undaunted. "Not since Daddy died."

The radio crackled for attention. Garrett grabbed up the mike as if it were a life preserver.

THE SWING was where Rachel did her best thinking. Its rhythm was a metronome for her feelings and expressions. The squeaking of the chain seemed an exclamation point to her thoughts. Even as a young girl she had sought solace in the swing when, to her young mind, she had been forced to live a hermit's existence.

She glanced at her daughters. They were content, using sticks to draw a playhouse in the still-damp earth around a tree stump. Having each other, they did not appear to suffer as she had from the isolation. Was still suffering, she thought, especially when she had a spare moment, like now, to let things sprout in her mind.

Her eyes strayed to the station wagon. Without moving an inch the old heap had caused her considerable dismay. Now, she had to figure out a way to ask Garrett to get her some gas. And still keep her pride intact.

Before she could form a plan beyond out-and-out asking, Garrett was pulling into the yard and Pete was charging up the stoop.

"Mom! Guess what! We answered a distress call. A tourist and his family camping in the forest got attacked by wild dogs! I helped rescue them! They had a girl dog in heat and the wild dogs came sniffing and the man tried to chase them away and he got bit. I held the tourniquet on his arm while Sheriff Stark drove him to Doc Williams's clinic. It was great! You should've seen the blood!"

"That's . . . that's nice," Rachel said to Pete, but her eyes were lit with anger as they settled on Garrett.

"We were almost heroes, but Sheriff Stark said it was just routine."

"I'll bet he did. You go wash up now. We were waiting on you to have supper."

Garrett tried explaining. "It wasn't as gory as he makes out. A couple of drops—"

"I suppose you think that's macho, taking my son out and . . . and exposing him to danger and I don't know what all—"

"Hold on, Rachel. He wasn't in any danger and I think it was good for him to see how things go in an emergency. As for danger, you've got more of it up here. Those wild dogs roam these mountains. Look how you keep the doors open on your place. They could be inside your house and on top of you before you know it."

"You're just trying to scare me." She spun around and called Caroline and Sara. "Hey, you two, in the house. Wash up for supper."

"I'm not hungry," announced Caroline. "I don't want to listen to Pete gloat all during supper."

"Go wash!" ordered Rachel.

"I'll be glad when I'm grown-up and the boss," Caroline sniffed. "C'mon, Sara, she means you, too."

When Rachel turned back to Garrett, he was grinning. "That little snit takes after her mama."

Rachel opened her mouth to rage at him, then remembered the empty gas tank. "Caroline is very sensitive. She hides it behind a saucy mouth."

Garrett took a half turn in the direction of his car.

"Wait!" Rachel called in a headlong fluster. "I mean . . . where're you going?" Oh, damn! If only she could just spit it out: I'm out of gas. Could you spare a gallon? But the asking of it lodged in her throat like a bone.

"I left two deputies scouting the woods for signs of those dogs. Have to check on them."

Rachel's flustered state suddenly led to an offer she hadn't planned to make. "Would—would you like to take supper with us?"

Something inside Garrett leaped a little, yet he was instantly wary. The simple invitation seemed to encompass countless hopes. His eyes slid down to Rachel's toes and up again. "You're making an actual invitation?"

"It's just fried chicken, gravy, biscuits and vegetables out of the garden. I thought since you had Pete out all day..."

Hands on his hips, Garrett rocked on his heels, studying Rachel, considering the invitation. She was changing her tune too quickly to suit him. She was up to something, being so suddenly soft-spoken, so suddenly demure. He could credit his charm with working wonders, but he had already been thinking charisma wasn't the road to Rachel. Supper was bait. A lure, like a piece of high-smelling meat in a coyote trap. "I am hungry," he admitted, feeling her out. "We were about to wheel into Nester's when the distress call came through."

Rachel gave him a sweet smile. Garrett thought it smacked of entrapment. "That's settled, then. You can ask the blessing."

"Blessing? You mean, 'Amen, dig in'?"

"I'd hope for a bit more than 'Amen, dig in' from a man of your reputation."

She's going to poison me, Garrett thought, following Rachel to the table, every fiber of his being protesting. He mumbled through "Bless this house, Bless this food" and fiddled with his fork until Rachel looked at him inquiringly.

"I thought you were hungry. You're not eating."

Garrett tried a grin, feeling it go awry. "You've got the wings on your plate. I like those better than the thigh and breast."

"Well . . . here, trade plates with me."

"You're sure you don't mind?"

"Not at all. After all, you're my guest."

She sounded so sincere Garrett was flattered, and felt a tiny twinge of remorse for his earlier mean thoughts. He'd been spending too much time in the company of the bad guys. He was overly suspicious. Rachel was beginning to trust him. Maybe even like him.

A multitude of things competed for Rachel's attention as she served the children. Pete wanted gravy on his potatoes, Caroline wanted it on the biscuits. Sara wouldn't eat gravy at all. One wanted tea, two, milk. She forgot the salt. Pete, still high on excitement, had to be cautioned against talking with his mouth full. He ignored Sara who began to pout, and Rachel had to take the child on her lap and feed her from her own plate. Caroline was becoming insufferable, behaving with exaggerated poise.

While Garrett ate he watched the goings-on about the table with growing impatience. Rachel had hardly been able to swallow two mouthfuls of food. He wanted to slam his hand down on the table and order the children to behave so their mother could eat. When the children were finally excused to get their baths, he couldn't hold his exasperation back any longer. "How do you stand it?"

"Stand what?"

"All that confusion with the kids during dinner?" Her expression had changed before he finished the sentence. He knew he'd made a mistake, overstepping an imponderable boundary.

"I thought it went very well," she said stiffly.

He was too far in the war zone to back down now. Besides, she was wrong. "You let those scamps run roughshod over you. Jumping up and down to satisfy their every whim. Teach them to be independent, let them get their own tea, or salt, or whatever. And it wouldn't hurt for them to have a little respect for you." He eyed the cold congealed food on her plate. "You didn't get ten bites of your supper." He raised his eyes to her face, seeing not her anger, her hurt, but only the promise of sensuality so potent it was almost tangible. He had a sudden compulsive urge to grab her and drag her outside where he could . . . kiss some sense into her. Her breasts were fluttering lightly against her blouse, revealing her agitated state. His hands itched to cup one, then the other, feel that light quivering against his tough-skinned palms.

"You have no right—"

"Oh, hell! Who does?" He yanked a cigar out of his pocket, fiddling with it while his mind played with the vision of Rachel in his arms. "Listen, I've got to go. Thanks for feeding me."

He rose suddenly and stalked out the door.

Confusion mounted in Rachel. She couldn't let him leave, not until she had gas, enough anyway to get her to the station in Hickory Grove. He was halfway to his patrol car before she managed to call out. He stopped and Rachel stepped off the porch into the soft twilight left from a fading sun. "The station wagon . . . it's out of gas." She took several steps in his direction.

"Don't come any closer Rachel. I might do something you'll wish I hadn't." His features were hidden in a length of shadow. His tone was savage, but his voice was filled with restraint.

A chill raced up Rachel's spine, filling her with rage. "You started all this by coming here uninvited. I won't be—be put off by threats. You've tried to worm your way into my family, just to complain about me, my children. I get my fill of that with my mother-in-law. I'm doing the best I can with what I have. My children don't have anything going for them but me. The reason for that is your own negligence in doing your job!"

"I'm sick of you throwing Clive in my face. I suppose he was a perfect husband, a perfect father."

Rachel felt a sickening rush of pain. "He was my husband, Garrett, and he was the father of my children. And he is dead. You can't change that."

Garrett ran his fingers through his hair. "Why is it we always seem to end up arguing about Clive? I'll send a deputy out with a can of gas before he goes off duty tonight. Will that suit you?"

Rachel raised her chin. "Yes. Thank you."

"Thank you," he mimicked with cold sarcasm. "Sticks in your craw to say that to me, doesn't it?"

"It doesn't bother me a bit. You're just suffering from an overinflated ego."

With the deepening of twilight the chickens began flying up into the trees to roost. Nearby, one clucked loudly as if trumpeting the end of day. Garrett closed the distance to his car in several long strides. He jerked the car into motion and backed up until he was aligned with Rachel. "Night, ma'am," he uttered with ill-controlled fury.

"Make me happy, Garrett. Go wrap yourself around a tree."

He hung an elbow out the window. "I hate women who always think they have to have the last word."

5

HICKORY GROVE WAS UNINCORPORATED, with no mayor, no town government and no police. It was the county seat, with a courthouse, four commissioners, two judges, one justice of the peace, a high school, two elementary schools and three churches—Baptist, Methodist and Church of Christ, Scientist. The townsfolk of Hickory Grove thought that was about as much government as a body could bear. They didn't think it economical to pay for city services when Lackawanna County provided for their needs so splendidly. A three-block shopping district on Main Street furnished a drugstore, a department store, a Sears catalog order store, Buster's Feed and Seed with an auction barn behind it, a Chinese restaurant, Nester's Café and Red Circle Grocery. A small lumber mill stood just beside the sign that marked the town's entrance from the south. The trees for which the town had been named a hundred years earlier had long ago had their bark removed and been cut into boards there. Hickory Grove's northern border was marked by a bait shop and a dozen rustic cabins—a tourist's haven.

Prosperity might have once looked in on Hickory Grove, but look was all it did in passing. The little town's one redeeming feature was that it was nestled in the wide crook of a pair of majestic Ozark mountains. The highway heading north would take you all the way to Kansas City, Missouri, and south to Hot Springs and then on to Louisiana. The sounds and smells from the auction barn on Tuesdays could make you dig for a handkerchief to put over your nose, but Hickory Grove was proud, litter free, and the garden society kept the thoroughfares trimmed and planted with blooming shrubs.

The sheriff's office and jail were housed in a squat building on a lot behind the courthouse square. Chewing the stub of a cigar and leaning back in his chair, his feet propped on the much-scarred desktop, Garrett Stark was aware of a number of things. First was his weariness, which did not conflict with the knowledge that his body was strong and his muscles hard. Then there was the smell of leather and gun oil, and the rank odor of smoke and stale sweat that no amount of disinfectant ever penetrated. He was aware, too, of the sounds coming from the jail kitchen, which was down the hall behind him.

A jail trustee was preparing the meals for inmates in the lockups. Of the dozen and a half prisoners, only two were from Lackawanna County. The rest were overflow from a neighboring county that paid Lackawanna handsomely to house their prisoners. Most were drunks or traffic violators sitting out their fines. Garrett refused to accept outside inmates convicted of violence of any kind. Lackawanna County was too small and too poor to maintain a major county prison system. Those folk convicted of misdemeanors were given a liberal option by county judges to pay their fines. Those convicted of felonies were remanded to the state prison. Garrett liked it that way.

He made a mental note to check the sugar. Jail cook Billy Bass—wizened, toothless and hairless—was an old-time bootlegger. Let Billy get his hands on a pound of sugar and an apple or an ear of corn, and he'd have a pot of liquor brewing somewhere. Twice in the past six weeks Billy had been too drunk to cook. But the sounds coming from the kitchen now had a steady rhythm: quiet stirring, lids being lifted and replaced, Billy whistling some tuneless toothless melody. When he was drunk he bellowed spirituals at the top of his lungs.

Garrett turned his thoughts to other more pressing things—he settled on Rachel Cameron.

He wished he could make her understand that Clive's suicide had not been an event that he or anyone, even Rachel, could have predicted. It had been and still was his policy to let the prisoners out of their cells to eat their meals at the long narrow table in the kitchen where Billy served them. It was more efficient and, Garrett thought, more humane than shoving plates beneath the bars of the cells.

He had taken Clive Cameron into custody in the late afternoon, and Clive had refused to leave his cell to eat. While all the other prisoners were dining, Clive had hung himself. He had fashioned a noose from strips of his shirt, tied the other end to the high crossbeam on the cell bars and leaped from the top bunk. His neck had snapped and he died instantly.

No one had been more stricken with remorse than Garrett. Now he told himself that was why he was taking such an avid interest in Clive Cameron's family. He was suffering by degrees emotions of pity, of tenderness, and the desire to . . .

He wasn't in love. Absolutely not. He had no taste for marriage. Rachel just needed looking after until she got on her feet. Any sensitive, caring man like himself

could understand that. He didn't mind doing the looking after. And anybody in his right mind could see she
needed a hand with those kids. Pete needed the firm
guidance of a man. Caroline . . . well, that was one kid
whose caustic tongue needed a rubdown with soap.
And Sara. There was a puzzle. Doing all her talking
through Pete. Laziness or anger, or just plain stub-
bornness like her mother . . .

Damn! When he was away from Rachel he could
build in his mind all kinds of witty conversations. Five
minutes in her presence and they were at each other's
throats. It was the name-calling that did it. Saying he
was devious, immoral, egotistical . . . Then he recalled
that his marine buddies had called one another the vil-
est names. In camaraderie. In affection. Maybe that
meant she really liked him, he thought, hope rising. He
just hadn't been taking it right.

He needed only to keep in mind that Rachel was a
woman, that she was susceptible to attention, even to
flattery. A few well-placed words and Rachel might
open all her private doors to him.

He conjured up the memory of her standing before
him that first day—wet, blouse clinging, tanned flesh,
shapely legs, eyes sparking. And that evening a week
ago, when her breasts were quivering.

A warm feeling cascaded all around him as he stood
up and stretched. He recognized, arriving at that recognition with impatience, even annoyance, that he had
to have Rachel Cameron. The problem, he thought,
would be getting her alone. A man couldn't make love
to a woman with three kids hanging on to her shirttail.

RACHEL CAME OUT of the Hickory Grove post office, her
hands trembling with the registered letter from the So-

cial Security Administration. Two months after Clive's death she had applied for benefits for the children. She had filled out reams and reams of questionnaires, provided birth certificates, her marriage certificate, Clive's employment records . . . She hoped and prayed that inside the envelope there was a check. It would keep them going until she got her contract to teach. Once money of her own began to come in, she would be able to bank the social security checks for the children, for college, for vacations, a nest egg for each of them to start their own lives.

"What'd we get, Mom?" asked Pete when she slid behind the wheel of the station wagon.

"A business letter. Be quiet while I read it." It wasn't a check. Her heart sank. Somehow they had misplaced Clive's death certificate. Would she please send another. Today was Saturday, and all the county offices were closed. Another delay. Rachel sighed, folded the letter and put it in her purse. "Grocery store next, kids."

"Afterward, can we go to Nester's for hamburgers?"

"No. For what that'd cost, I can feed us three or four meals. But I'll buy the makings and we can have them at home. Okay?"

"I hate being poor!" said Caroline.

"Don't we all," replied her mother.

"Well, can we go see Grandma Cameron before we go home?"

"You're asking all the impossibles today, Caroline. You know your grandmother insists we give her a day's notice before we visit. Besides, we'll have milk and butter in the car. We can't leave it in the heat. And, as it is, it'll be near dark when we start for home. You know I hate driving at night."

"You just don't like Grandma Cameron!" Folding her arms over her thin chest, Caroline leaned back in a huff.

There was enough truth in her daughter's words to make Rachel wince. The dislike between herself and Adele Cameron was mutual. But Rachel prided herself on making an effort to be pleasant for the children's sake. Adele Cameron was their only grandparent. From the very first, Adele had blamed Rachel for Clive's lack of success, blamed Rachel for his dropping out of college. And Rachel had been too loyal to her husband to tell Adele the truth—that Clive had been expelled from the University of Arkansas, had taken odd jobs in Fayetteville in order to remain near her. Rachel had refused to marry him until she had her degree. It had come in handy, too, that first year before Pete was born. She had worked as a teacher's aide in Hickory Grove, and the money had supplied the down payment on their home. Now she eyed Caroline's frown in the rearview mirror. "Tell you what. We'll call your grandmother from the grocery store and invite ourselves for Monday. You can visit her while I take care of some business at the courthouse."

"I'd rather go over to the jail and see Sheriff Stark," announced Pete. "He said anytime I dropped by I could earn two dollars sweeping out his office."

Rachel tensed, annoyed. "You're never to take money from him, you hear?"

"Can't I take money for work? I asked him for a job."

But it wouldn't be a real job, Rachel knew. It would be charity. She'd put a stop to that the next time she saw Garrett. The next time . . . She felt a jolt of apprehension, as if the thoughts and dreams she'd had of Garrett could be pulled out for all to see. Thoughts and pictures she had not the strength or the will to chase from her mind while her pulse was spinning so. For a moment, she rested her arms on the steering wheel, seeing but not seeing the midsummer languor pervading the tiny mountain town. Then a westward-drooping sun slanted into her eyes, reminding her of the time. She fumbled for the keys in the ignition. "Grocery store, next stop," she said. Her voice was husky.

JUST AS TWILIGHT ENDED and plunged the mountain into gnarled shadows, Rachel turned off the paved highway onto the dirt lane that wound around to her lonely little house. The headlights were feeble illumination, emphasizing the dark that closed about the car. The anxiety at being so isolated—anxiety she usually managed to keep behind her—crept up and rode with her over the rutted path. She felt an incessant urge to hurry for the safety of the tiny clearing, knowing she didn't dare because of the sharp turns and switchbacks.

Sara lay on the front seat beside her, asleep, her thumb in her mouth. Pete and Caroline, in the back, argued over who was the strongest, who could carry the heaviest sack of groceries.

Rachel eased the car to a stop beneath the mulberry tree, turning off the ignition but staying her hand before she cut the lights, waiting for the tension to drain out of her.

The beams seemed to catch dimly a fluttering in the yard. Pete and Caroline began to scramble out of the car, unlocking doors. Something was awry. Rachel didn't know what exactly, but something made her stay them. "Wait a minute, kids. Close the doors." She could hear her voice, low, hoarse, alarmed.

"What is it, Mama?" Caroline had picked up at once Rachel's fright, which was reflected in her face.

"Shhhh." Rachel leaned her head out the window, listening with every fiber of her being, eyes straining to see beyond the narrow beams of the headlights.

She heard no sound. No fluttering of wings of chickens roosting in trees, no owls hooting, no frogs singing down by the creek, no crickets humming. She knew the silence then for what it was. A large animal, a mountain lion, a bear, though they were scarce, was stalking prey, hunting, and every creature in the forest had fallen into protective silence.

She closed her eyes for a split second, not so much relieved as succumbing to her common sense. She started the engine again and drove the station wagon right up to the front steps. She felt a tire press something soft. A toy, one of Sara's dolls. But as she stepped cautiously out of the car the inside light revealed one of the chickens. Or what was left of it. She felt a little sick. As a youngster she had never been able to help her parents with the slaughtering of the farm animals they had raised. She had always run and hidden from the stench of hot blood as it poured into the ground. And now, recognizable as no other, that same stench pervaded the air.

Suddenly, night noises began to rustle all about them. Rachel almost screamed. She raced around the car, up the steps, hurrying to open the huge unwieldy lock, her hand connecting with the light switch. Welcome light poured onto the porch. Everything was normal again. Except for the dead chicken, and Rachel put that out of her mind. A badger or a skunk got it, she was sure.

"I call the bathroom first!" hollered Caroline, racing past Rachel and Pete.

"I called it first!" Pete shouted, but Caroline had outmaneuvered him.

"Go 'round the corner of the porch," Rachel told him as she carried the still-sleeping Sara into the house.

"If she was a boy, I'd tear into her!"

"Well, she isn't. She's your sister, and I don't like violence. So, no fighting." Rachel moved to turn on every light in the house, over the sink, over the table, by the sofa, the lamp on her small dresser. She couldn't keep from taking a quick peek under her bed. She laughed at herself.

She heard a choking sound.

"Mama."

Pete stood at the threshold of the house, the blood drained from his face, his eyes flaring wide with fear. His tennis shoes tracked the floor as he took a step forward.

There was the unmistakable odor of offal. Rachel's throat closed and the back of her neck shrunk with horror.

She never remembered closing the space between them, screaming for Caroline, yanking the shoes from Pete's feet or slamming the door and bolting it.

"Something got my pig. Scared me when I saw it, but I'm okay, now."

"Well, I'm not," said Rachel, washing her hands and splashing cool water on her flushed hot face. She passed a cool cloth to Pete. "Here, wipe your face. You'll feel better."

"If I'da seen it in the daylight, I wouldn't have been scared."

Rachel dreaded seeing the carnage in the daylight. Worse, she dreaded the night to come. The smell of offal would bring every hungry wild animal from miles away. "You two go upstairs and get into your pajamas, and stay up there while I bring in the groceries."

An hour later, Rachel sat in the dark in a chair pulled up to the screened window. Moonlight trickled into the clearing, laying a path down to the creek. Nothing moved in the golden light. Her gaze flicked from shadow to shadow, watching, listening with her eyes as well as her ears. Tiny sounds of scuffling, squeaks, claws being sharpened on tree trunks made her stiffen. Part of her mind dwelled on the children. Pete and Caroline had caught her fright, had not been hungry for the hamburgers they had looked forward to. Only Sara, who had slept through it all, had had an appetite. The other part of her mind was obsessed with the knowledge that if they had arrived home five minutes sooner . . . interrupting the carnage . . . If—if anything had happened to herself, to her children, no one would have heard their screams.

She lit a cigarette, closing her eyes against the match to preserve her night vision.

The moon disappeared behind clouds. The night crept closer. She would not let the darkness frighten her: it was the same clearing in which she had grown up, the same clearing that she now walked across a dozen times a day, the trees were the same trees, the underbrush the same underbrush in which the chickens scratched. Something in the shadows fluttered and clicked. A dark shadow, darker than the rest, grotesque in shape, a living presence, came out of the forest and slithered across the porch. A scream rose from deep in Rachel's belly, exploding in her paralyzed throat. No sound came out.

GARRETT TURNED OFF the highway onto the dirt track that led to Rachel's house. He stopped the car, turned off the motor, lit a cigar and continued the argument he'd been having with himself. See Rachel. Don't see Rachel. He'd already lost that part. He had to see her. Now for the reason. Any excuse would do. Say he was just checking to see if his deputy had delivered the gas he'd sent. She'd see through that in a wink. He'd seen that same deputy every day for a week now. Could've checked with him. Which he had.

He could tell her he missed her. No. She'd get the wrong idea. He sure couldn't say how his stomach got all airy when he thought about her. That was sissy. And mentioning the ache in his groin would scare her off. He couldn't say how he wanted her naked so he could touch her thrusting breasts, touch the secret moist parts of her, taste the sweetness of her lips. The cigar burned unsmoked until ashes fell down his shirt. He brushed them away, and with the ashes went the pictures in his mind. Hell, he was acting like a fool. He was the sheriff. He didn't need excuses to go anywhere in the county. But he couldn't deny Rachel's pull. She was somehow summoning him to this mountainside.

He started the car, taking the switchbacks slowly until he eased to a stop in the yard. His hand went to the light switch, but a movement caught his eye. A low gray shape scuttled out of the beams of light before he could identify it. Suddenly, the porch light clicked on, the great thick door of the house was thrown open and Rachel was calling to him.

And then he was moving toward her in a sudden panic because her voice was strange, uneven, turning back on itself.

"Rachel! What's wrong? What's happened?"

"Thank God," she was murmuring. "Thank God...." Her knees began to give way. She swayed. Garrett slipped an arm about her. Holding her trembling sup-

ple length against his own enthralled him. He inhaled
the fragrance of her. Soap and sun . . . and the smell of
fear accosted his nostrils. He held her close.

Rachel was mumbling something incomprehensi-
ble, her voice low and intense; Garrett knew from experience she was trying to speak through shock and
relief. Finally, reluctantly, he had to pry her fingers from
his shirt and guide her across the dark room to the sofa.
He switched on the lamp and pulled up a chair to sit and
face her. Her gray-green eyes were glazed and there was
a spot of color high on each cheek. He took her small
hands into his great ones. "Now, start from the beginning."

It took Rachel a moment to focus on him, his weath-
ered face filled with concern, his eyes alight with curi-
osity and more. Her gaze dropped to her hands cupped
tightly in his and that was the moment she became
wholly aware of his virility, his strength, the ultimate
need in him. Something rapid and electric passed
through her. Rachel felt it pulsating as if the sensation
was trying to thrust itself between layers of her flesh,
trying to embed itself within her very core. She had to
tear her eyes away from his hands before she could
speak. "We went grocery shopping.... It was dark when
we got home. I saw . . . there're dead chickens all over
the yard. At first, I thought a skunk . . . But I couldn't
smell it. Then Pete—" She tried not to dwell on what
was out there. It frightened her too much. "I mean,
something gutted the pig. And then it came back. I
couldn't see what it was."

"Pete. What about Pete?" Garrett looked to the loft.
"Are the kids okay?"

"Yes. They're not hurt, but we all got scared."

"You just sit here . . . On second thought, why don't you make us coffee? I'll go outside and have a look around."

She pulled her hands from his. "You'll be careful?"

"Very."

It was totally irrational, there was no reason, no explanation for it, but after Garrett left the house to reconnoiter the clearing, Rachel gave up her fears and succumbed to the treacherous sensations that had been pounding her, dumbfounding her. Garrett was an uninvited intruder into her life. He had been since he'd come to her to tell her of Clive's death. She was appalled at the extent of her feelings for him, ashamed of herself at the same time. In one way she was anxious for Garrett to touch her so the wondering would be over. In another, she moved in a dreamy unreality that he might never do so. She tried to focus on her other life, *before widowhood*. Tried to recall what it was like to be kissed, to be held in another's arms, to be loved. The image eluded her. It had been too long. She went to make coffee, an ordinary act, an everyday occurrence. Rational.

When Garrett returned, Rachel felt her face still flaming with her thoughts, and she greeted him unsteadily.

"What did you find?"

"A mess. It's those dogs that the tourist had a run-in with, I think. Tracks look like it." He switched off his flashlight and put his shotgun on safety, leaning it against the wall. "They might come back. I'd better stay the night." Out of the corner of his eye he watched her reaction. Her expression was one of . . . acceptance? Despair? And he could not avoid noticing, too, how flushed her face was, how she was looking at him.

There was a silence, more tender than awkward. Garrett was still as stone, mesmerized by her smoldering eyes, chestnut hair spilling loose over her frail shoulders, and the juices of sex now pouring into his belly. Not to linger there, but shooting inexorably lower.

"Well," said Rachel, "would you like a cup of coffee?"

Garrett didn't think or plan. He closed the space between them, took the cup from Rachel's hand and placed it on the counter. "I don't want coffee."

"You said . . ." Staring at him, her voice trailed into nothingness.

"I know what I said," he stated, reaching for her, taking her by the shoulders and pulling her near him. "But this is what I really want . . ." And he bent his head, his lips hovering over hers for a second or two, or perhaps it was a lifetime. He repeated throatily, "This is what I want . . ."

His lips brushed hers lightly, once, twice, tasting the nectar he found there, holding back to prolong the exquisiteness of it all. "Rachel . . ." he breathed softly.

She was too overwhelmed to speak. The taste and feel of him was creating havoc within her. Tobacco. He had been sucking on a lemon drop. The gentle touch of his cool firm lips, his fingers biting into her shoulders, the length of his khaki-clad body so close. And yet, not close enough. It had been so long. Her breath dipped shallowly. She couldn't refuse. She wanted to be kissed, held, loved again, wanted . . . to reach the pinnacle. Her eyes, already heavy lidded with desire, closed entirely and Garrett pressed his lips to her lids, then kissed the tiny blue vein that throbbed in her temple.

If her brain was shouting, "No! No! No!" her body wasn't listening for it was alive with surging sensuality and it leaned into Garrett's with wild abandon.

An urgent moan broke from him, and then his mouth was upon hers, devouring, his hot tongue thrusting, breaching her lips, withdrawing, and the rhythm of it was more, much more than a kiss.

His arms were about her, crushing her to him so that she was aware of the taut straining hardness between his legs as it pressed and throbbed, searing against her soft thighs.

Rachel had not thought beyond the kiss. She had to now for her insides felt the old tenseness and expectation, and she tried prying her lips from Garrett's. But he refused to let her go. Finally, finally his mouth began a path to the soft fragrant hollow in her throat, and she was able to speak in a ragged breathless voice. "Stop, Garrett . . . please . . . stop."

"Feels too good to stop," he murmured, and didn't. She could feel puffs of warm breath on her neck. It sent shivers down her spine. He felt them, tracing their patterns with his strong fingers.

She was dizzy with a sense of unreality. Yet his lips, his moist tongue, the swelling at the juncture of his thighs that was pressing insistently against her were very real. Undeniably real. She drew in a great gulp of air. "No more, please. The children might wake up."

He lifted his head, looking at her, saw her stricken expression. Though he had left off kissing her he could not keep his hands from her. Lightly, almost reverently, he trailed the tip of a finger from the pulsating hollow in her throat to the seductive rise of her silken breasts. Rachel gripped his hand before it could explore further. "We have to stop."

Garrett wanted to forge his way into her body, certain now that it would welcome him. "You don't want to stop and I don't, either." He was exercising control, but at great cost. "Check on them. They're probably sound asleep."

"I know they're asleep. It's just . . . it's more than just them. Kissing is one thing. You—you want more." Common sense prevailed. She couldn't do more with Garrett, not in a million years. Bedding him would be parallel to the poor man who invited the rich man to eat the last scrap of food upon his table. And then the poor man died of hunger, betrayed by his own impracticality. Besides, the hostility she felt toward him could not be shed like a chrysalis in one night of kissing and touching.

"I'd say that's obvious." Garrett's tone mocked the passion straining within him, allowing it to fade, but the fierce light in his eyes remained.

A maddening hot flush washed over Rachel's face. She turned away, retrieving Garrett's cup from the counter, her own from a shelf. "You can't stay the night here, not now."

The tension between them was wire taut and each knew it.

"The conviction in your voice wouldn't turn away a flea. What's so sacred, Rachel? We're neither virgins, we're both alone. We both need release." He hadn't meant it quite that way, but the spark in her eyes was undeniable. It set every part of him on fire.

Her deep gray-green eyes, fixed so intently on Garrett, suddenly glowed. "No! I don't—I don't need . . ." she faltered, going quiet. Every bone in her face stood out under her flesh. She did not look away from him for an instant.

They were braced a few feet apart now, sipping coffee, neither daring to move to the table or the sofa to sit. The big old bed was in the periphery of vision. Rachel shifted her stance, putting it firmly behind her.

"Rachel, what I'm feeling, what you're feeling won't disappear, you know."

"I don't know what you mean."

"Now we're into fairy tales. Let me spell it out for you. You're hungry for a man." *Not just any man,* he thought, *but me.* "You have needs that you can't ignore. They won't be put on a back burner for long, not without flaring up." For a moment he closed his eyes, looking inward.

"You don't have to say any more—"

"Oh, but I want to. We have chemistry, you and I—"

"No, we don't. And I don't fancy just becoming another of your...women."

He held the silence for what seemed like forever. His smile got tighter and tighter. At last he said, "Ah! You just wanted to see if you could get to the head of the line?"

"No!"

"You're shouting," he said, half in disgust. "You'll wake the children."

"Leave them out of this," she whispered, feeling as though her bones were turning to chalk.

Garrett expelled the merest breath of a sigh. "You brought them into it. All I wanted—"

"I know what you wanted." Her cup rattled on the counter as she put it down.

"Well, damn me to hell and back. What are you suddenly? A saint? You want. I want. We were on the same wavelength. Still are, if you'd be honest enough to admit it."

"I'm not admitting anything. You're using police tactics on me."

He almost gasped. "Now that's what I call bearing false witness."

Rachel's frustration was bringing her very close to tears. She hugged herself to still her trembling, but her own arms reminded her of Garrett's wrapped around her. Her breasts, yearning for his touch, had not yet stopped humming with erotic currents. She dropped her arms, holding them stiffly at her sides. "I can manage by myself now. I'm not frightened anymore. If it's just dogs . . ."

Garrett stared at her face. Rachel was looking at him so strangely, as if there were something he should know. He couldn't read her mind. A man was crazy to trust half of what a woman said, and downright stupid if he imagined he could deduce what was going on in her head. "Not 'just dogs.' A pack of snarling, mean, wild beasts. A half-dozen farmers have been trying to track them for a week for killing calves." He flung his hand in the direction of the doorway, where he had left the door open to encourage a cooling breeze. "And they attacked that tourist, remember?"

Rachel paled considerably. Garrett pulled out a cigar, casually began unwrapping it. Maybe he'd gone too far. He liked her. But even if you like someone, he thought, and that someone makes you angry, you feel like getting even. He was more than angry right now. He had a lusty ache in his groin and a pair of aspirin sure as hell wasn't the cure.

"Do you think the dogs'll come back?" Her emotions were like mercury, slithering every which way, impossible to harness.

"They might. They might not."

"You could leave me that shotgun."

"You know how to use a gun?"

"No. My mother threw all of ours into the creek after Daddy fell over his and died. But you could show me."

"Too dangerous. You might accidentally hurt yourself. Or one of the kids."

Rachel had been thinking that, too. She hated guns. Clive had had guns, but he'd stored them at his mother's. Rachel wouldn't let one in the house—until now. She lifted her hand in a gesture of futility. "I'll just have to lock up tight after you leave."

"You're certain you want me to go?" He knew she was. She was cloaking herself in brave dignity, a substance as impenetrable as iron. He sighed. "All right, if you want to bury yourself out here like a fossil . . ."

He helped her secure the screened windows, the front and side doors, feeling a bit lost when he found himself on the porch, locked out. Before he left he went around the yard and pigpen once again, coming upon nothing more frightening than a baby possum. Hell, he'd have to assign a deputy to watch the place, quietly and out of sight. Angling back to his cruiser, he noted Rachel had turned off the porch light again.

"Garrett!" The unexpected sound of her softly calling voice startled him. Hope leaped in his breast and his eyes burned brightly as if refueled.

"What?"

"Good night," came quietly across the clearing.

Garrett lifted his hand in response and with difficulty turned away. The resolution he had made to himself earlier that day in his office came slamming back into his mind. He had to have Rachel Cameron. *Where there's a will, there's a way. An old cliché*, he thought. However, he was willing, and Rachel was willing whether she admitted it or not. Finding the *way* was troublesome. But, hell, what was a little trouble if you were on the path to bliss? His disposition cheering, Garrett spent the twenty-minute drive into town willing away the not unpleasant bone hardness that plagued him.

It was well past midnight when Rachel kicked off her espadrilles and lay down on her bed. She flung an arm out, touching the pillow next to her. What would it have been like, she thought, to fling her arm like that and find Garrett? She indulged her senses, reliving the moments in his arms, the feel of his lips on hers, the thrusting of his tongue that was so like...so like... Oh, she was withering inside. She would never be a whole woman again!

The moon, moving into its equinox, cast a thick pale glow into the house. Above her head, Rachel heard the hushed echoes of footfalls, and marked their progress across the loft and down the stairs to her side. She took Sara into her bed, cooing softly, cuddling her.

She had done the right thing, she told herself. Sending Garrett away. She had. Much later, her eyes swimming with weariness, she slipped into a restless sleep.

6

RACHEL LOST THE PICTURE of the dream when she awakened. But not its essence. Somehow the dream had focused on the parallel of her life and that of her mother's.

Widowed at twenty-seven when Rachel herself was only eight, Mattie Wallis had become taciturn, folding her life in on itself by existing purposefully within the humdrum Wallis homestead. Unable to afford feelings. Unable to afford to acknowledge how much she wanted a life filled with gaiety. Perhaps another man. Mattie's entire world had focused on Rachel, wanting for her daughter what she herself had longed for—education, storybook marriage, happiness. Rachel felt guilty now for having never suspected, for having taken Mattie and the life she had led for granted.

Mattie had been filled to bursting when Rachel finished college, thrilled when Rachel had been a teacher's aide at Oak Grove Elementary School, thinking her daughter's future assured. After Pete's birth Mattie had encouraged Rachel to return to work. "I'll baby-sit Pete, you keep your hand in over at the school. You never can tell when you'll need work."

"I'm different from you, Mama." Rachel winced now, recalling those words. "Besides, Clive will take care of us. I don't want to work right now. I want to enjoy being a mother."

"You'll always be a mother. Work . . . well, that ain't so easy to come by," Mattie retorted, but she hadn't said anything more. Then, while Rachel was pregnant with Sara, Mattie had died in her sleep. Content? Rachel wondered. Her mother seemed to come from memory into reality, seemed to enter Rachel's presence, and Rachel saw now that between them was a sharing that death had not touched. She understood so much about her mother now.

Could I, Rachel asked herself, be content to live my life through my children? She couldn't. She knew she couldn't. Especially since Garrett had touched her.

She had enjoyed his caresses, the giddy anticipatory rush that had swelled within her, and the painful relentless longing that even now was so potent that parts of her burned with desire.

She needed someone, she thought. A helpmate. She wished she could peer into the future to know what she had to look forward to. On one count, she knew. No guessing there. She was solely responsible for the three lives she had brought into the world. Responsible, trapped and terrified. She swallowed, pushing down the panic. As she drew her knees up she discovered that Sara was using her legs and hips as a brace for a line of dolls.

Through a thin slit of lashes she watched her daughter soundlessly mouth words to the dolls, chastising them, calling them by name. Charlie? Christine? Casper? Rachel only recognized the shaping of "Miss Mossy," for Miss Mossy, bedraggled and decrepit, had been one of her own dolls, and she had introduced Miss Mossy to Sara. "Say 'good morning' to Mama, Sara," Rachel encouraged. In her own fashion, Sara did, kissing Rachel soundly, then the child held all of her babies up for a kiss, too. "Enough!" Rachel said with a laugh after a moment, propping herself up with pillows to contemplate her daughter. "Sara, Sara," she whispered, "couldn't you say 'mama' just once?" But Sara had gone back to her dolls, gone back into her own silent world.

So small and in need of so much, thought Rachel. Each day of Sara's silence left her somehow defeated. There were so many uncertainties in life and dealing with the possibilities of Sara's future left her exhausted. But how could she possibly predict Sara's future when her own contained problems and challenges she'd never dreamed of?

A car door slammed, punctuating the quiet of early morning. Rachel sat up, and all the horror of the evening before returned in a rush. The dead pig, the chickens lying about the yard . . .

Garrett had returned! Closing her eyes for a moment, Rachel saw a very clear detailed image of herself and Garrett making love. She felt a pang of guilt and chagrin at the image. How could she even imagine that?

When she looked out the window, it wasn't the sheriff but one of his deputies and a truckload of prisoners clothed in jail garb. Her disappointment was so strong it was like something bitter on her tongue.

Anxious, inquisitive, she brushed her hair, washed her face and, smoothing the clothes in which she'd slept, went to open the front door.

"Hey, Rachel!" the deputy said, approaching the porch. "Remember me? Slim Walters?"

Slim Walters wasn't slim now. He was rotund, balding, smiling, and Rachel couldn't place him. Her blank expression told him so.

"William Walters. I graduated a year ahead of you, then I went into the Navy."

"Oh, oh yes. Billy Walters. Susan's brother." Vaguely she remembered Susan Walters coming to school with eyes tear-stained and swollen because her favorite brother had joined the Navy behind his family's back. Susan was now living somewhere in California in a commune, or so the gossip had it.

"Right."

"You're out of the service?"

"Yep, the wife was tired of moving around, wanted to settle the kids in one place."

Rachel smiled over her anxiety, and eyed the six men still sitting in the back of the pickup. "What—"

"Volunteers. We're going to clean up this mess around your place. Get rid of the carcasses. Cut back some of the underbrush crowding the yard."

"You don't have to—"

"Sheriff's orders. Besides, it's not a pleasant sight for the squeamish, or for your kids."

"I . . . no, it isn't."

Slim turned to go, stopping in midstride. "Say, there's still some haunch and side left on the pig. You want us to finish butchering it for you? Salt it down?"

Bile rose in Rachel's throat. "It was almost a pet. Pete was going to sell him after the county fair in October. We couldn't possibly eat him."

Slim shook his head. "Too bad. Hope we find those dogs soon. They're tearing up the county."

"Slim, wait. Is it safe? With the prisoners, I mean?"

"Oh, sure. They're regulars. Bunch of drunks mostly, getting sober on county time."

"And Sheriff Stark? He's coming, too?" She hadn't meant to ask. Hadn't meant to let his name cross her lips. But there it was, said.

Slim shrugged. "He didn't say. Well, we'd better get to working so we'll be finished before lunch. These guys don't like to miss a meal."

"What's going on, Mom?" Pete peered around Rachel, wiping sleep from his eyes.

"A clean-up crew, is all. The sheriff sent them."

"My pig, I guess," replied Pete, sounding forlorn.

"I'm sorry about your pig. Maybe we can get another one later."

"But not in time for the fair?"

"No, not in time for the fair." Taking Pete by the hand, Rachel pulled him into the house and onto the sofa. "I wish you didn't have to learn about disappointment so early in life, Pete. I wish I could make it different, but I can't. I know you were counting on that pig winning a ribbon and some auction money."

"I wanted the money for all of us, not just me."

"I know, and I'm proud of you for that."

"Anyway?"

"Anyway. You have a good heart, and that counts more with me than any old pig."

"There's a whole bunch of prisoners in our backyard," yelled Caroline, hanging over the loft railing.

"Keep your voice down, Caroline, or they'll hear you," cautioned Rachel. She began to think it would be a good idea to get the children away from the farm while the work crew was there.

"I'm sure they already know they're prisoners," Caroline retorted, but quietly.

"No one likes to be reminded of their misfortune." Rachel began to bustle about, setting the table, heating the frying pan for bacon, filling the coffeepot. Now and again sounds drifted in the window on the slightest whisper of breeze: laughter, a sneeze, bits and pieces of conversation. "You know what I think we ought to do today?" she said to no one in particular. "We ought to go to church."

Pete sat up on the sofa, gazing at Rachel, thoughtful, assessing. "People who're good-hearted don't have to go, do they?"

Laughing, Rachel said, "Yes, they do. Sunday school helps keep them that way."

"See what you started," Pete directed glumly to his sister. "We finally get some excitement around here and we have to go off and leave it."

"NOW THAT WASN'T SO BAD, was it?" declared Rachel as she pulled out of the shady church parking lot into the crackling midday sun. "The air-conditioning was lovely. I'd almost forgotten . . ."

"It was nice seeing all my school friends again," agreed Caroline, her tone filled with wistfulness.

Rachel's heart contracted. Not once had she considered how lonely the children must have been feeling. In her mind she had been thinking that as long as they had each other they would be entertained. They were as lonely for companions their own age as she herself was.

Sara, not to be left out, waved a crayoned picture in front of her mother.

"Hey! Watch that, squirt, I can't see where I'm driving. Is that what you did in Sunday school?"

Sara nodded.

"Well, I can see it's a beautiful picture."

Pete leaned over the front seat and inspected the drawing. "It's Moses when he was a baby when his mother put him in a basket to float down the Nile."

"That was a terrible thing for his mother to do," countered Caroline. "A baby. He couldn't swim. Suppose his head went under the water?"

"Oh, you think everybody's a scaredy-cat when it comes to water," groused Pete.

"If we were meant to go under water, we'd have gills."

Pete groaned. "I suppose if we were meant to fly, we'd have wings instead of airplanes."

"Flying is different. You can breathe when you fly."

"You two take a page out of Sara's book for a change, and be quiet."

"Aw, Mom."

When the children settled down, Rachel became preoccupied with her own thoughts. Uppermost in her mind was Garrett, thoughts of whom made her throat tight, her body registering unwilling fascination with his maleness. She retreated from him, forcing herself instead to think of the coming week—Monday, to the courthouse; Tuesday, a letter to the school board reminding them of her application. If the weather held, on Wednesday she'd harvest the garden again for green beans and squash and maybe do some canning. And then there was the matter of the children being lonely. She'd have to figure out something, some way to have their little friends out to the mountain for an afternoon.

This mental to-do list made her feel good. Last evening had been one of panic and wild emotions. Tomorrow might be anything. Today was calm induced by church services, fragrant with sharp summer smells, and a gladdening sensation that, for the moment, all was right with her world. Rachel smiled to herself and hummed a spiritual that lingered in her mind.

"You going to pull over, Mama, or make him chase us?"

"Wha—?" Rachel glanced in the rearview mirror, her heart thudding as it sank into her stomach. A patrol car sped up behind her, its siren blaring two short bursts.

"It's Sheriff Stark," announced Pete, kneeling on the back seat for a better view. "He's waving to us. No, he's pointing to the shoulder. You better pull over, Mom. Maybe he wants to give us a ticket."

"Maybe he just wants to ruin my day," muttered Rachel.

"How can he do that?" Caroline wondered.

Just by breathing, thought Rachel. She maneuvered off the road, set the brake and leaped out of the car. "Now what?" She accosted Garrett the instant he emerged from his car, adjusting his hat brim against the bright sun.

"Is that any way to say hello on this cheery Sunday noon?"

"Your way is better? Turning on a siren and scaring me half to death?"

"It was hardly a squeak. I was just on my way to your place to see how the boys cleaned it up—"

"Don't you have anything better to do than dog me?"

The sheriff leaned against the fender of his patrol car, folded his arms across his chest and lazily tracked Rachel from head to toe, taking in her nylon-clad legs, the full beige skirt buttoned at her small waist, the white cotton blouse through which he could see her slip straps. Her glossy chestnut hair was pulled loosely atop her head, giving her stature. "You know, I don't understand you, Rachel. We did part friends last night."

"No, we didn't."

The brim of his old felt hat shaded his eyes, emphasizing their curious lightness. His smile was marvelous to behold. "Rachel Cameron that was you in my arms last night, that was you kissing me back, that was you—"

"Stop it," she demanded, cheeks flaring, recalling every wonderful erotic sensation. "The children might overhear."

Garrett dropped his gaze, studying the ground, seemingly intent on a rock he was worrying with one of his booted feet. "You can't hide behind those kiddies forever, my friend," he said, speaking amiably.

"I'm not hiding."

Then it came to him in a flash as bright as the hot wilting sun beating down upon them. Rachel's hostility was a sort of weapon against apprehension, against the roiling emotions she was trying to master, against him, for it was he who was stirring those emotions from a banked fire. The greater her violence of feeling for him, the greater would be her denial. He'd get around that, he promised himself. It was just a matter of bearing up until Rachel got sensible. "Did it ever occur to you that you're running away from life, and now you're running away from me, too? A regular little fossil you are, just waiting to be dug up."

"Somebody ought to dig *you* up and put you on the end of a fishhook."

"You like name-calling, don't you?"

"What do you want? Why did you want me to pull over?"

He unfolded his arms, jamming his hands into his pockets to better fight the urge he had to touch her, to draw her to him and revel in the bliss of her body melding with his. "How about going out to dinner with me?"

Rachel gaped. A part of her wanted to accept with alacrity. Just the thought of a couple of hours spent only in the company of another adult, with adult conversation, being able to eat a leisurely meal while having no childish squabbles to settle was so appealing, she almost said yes. She stared at Garrett, their eyes caught and held, and she was reminded of all the anguished frustrations of the past, the present, let alone what the future held. Going out to dinner with Garrett was tantamount to a date. A date with the man who had let her husband die. On the practical side, she had no babysitter, and if she had, no money to spare for such frivolity. "What happened last night has swelled your ego. Our... kissing was just one of those situations where relief causes an aberration of behavior. Especially mine. I admit it." She set her mouth stubbornly. "If that's all you wanted, I have to be going. It's hot in the car." She could see Pete's flushed face as he hung out a window. "Or did you want to issue me a ticket for some vague infraction of the law?"

"Aberration!" His voice rumbled with disbelief. "You've got the most mysteriously working female mind I've ever come across."

"That's probably because it isn't women's minds you're interested in."

"Well, this isn't getting us anywhere," concluded Garrett.

"That's best, don't you think?" Her smile was too tight to reflect anything except a snub.

He tipped his hat. "No ticket, ma'am," he said, so loftily respectful the sarcasm could not be missed. "Not even a warning."

Rachel returned to her car under the illusion that that was that. She was unhappy with the manner in which she had handled Garrett, yet proud that she had mustered the strength to resist temptation.

"What'd he want, Mom?"

"Just to say hello, Pete, that's all. Get your head back in the window. Somebody's liable to sideswipe us and take it off."

"Hold up a minute."

Rachel cried out in surprise. Leaning one arm on the roof of her car, Garrett had bent over and thrust his head in the window.

"Will you stop doing that?" she snapped.

"What?"

"Coming up on me like that. I thought you were back in your car."

"I just wanted to remind you to lock up tight every night. Don't let the kids wander around the forest until we catch those dogs."

"I have that much sense."

"I'm sure you do, but I'd be remiss in my elected duty if I didn't remind you . . . ma'am."

"Thank you," Rachel said icily, putting her foot to the gas pedal and driving off in a shower of gravel.

Caroline spoke accusingly. "The sheriff was making eyes at you, Mama. I saw him."

As if reality had touched her for the first time, Rachel glanced back at her daughter, eyes wide, face pale. "He was squinting against the sun."

"Well, I don't want another daddy. They fuss too much. Promise me we won't get another one," begged Caroline, as if in the whole seven years of her life, which included minuscule experience with men, she had already been tried beyond endurance.

If Caroline hadn't been so serious, Rachel would have laughed. As it was, she wanted to cry—for all that had not been and for all that would never be in her small family. A truth nagged at her. Clive *had* fussed an awful lot. Funny, she had forgotten. "I can't make a promise like that, Caro." And Rachel knew then, deep in her heart, why she couldn't. "But I'll always love you. I won't ever love anyone more than I love each of you." *Differently, perhaps,* she thought, *but never more.*

"You don't have to worry about Sheriff Stark being our daddy." So spoke Pete with the asperity of superior knowledge. "He's not ready to get married. He likes excitement. He told me."

Rachel experienced a curious tremor, almost a shiver. She wanted to ask what Pete had said to Garrett to provoke such a comment, but she was afraid his answer would mortify her. She was sure now she had been utterly correct to refuse Garrett's offer of dinner. Thank goodness she had said no last night! *Let him get his excitement from the waitresses down at Nester's,* she thought, trying valiantly to ignore a sagging disappointment.

After lunch Rachel found herself enduring a boredom she seldom suffered nowadays. She had half expected Garrett to follow her home, but he had not. It was too hot to iron or putter around in the garden. She didn't feel like doing any mending or washing. The long hot day seemed to go by in inches. The children, still high on the excitement of Sunday school and seeing their friends, were unmanageable. Finally she decided to defy danger, taking the children for a swim in the creek.

Sitting on the old log that spanned its width, she kept a sharp lookout and an ear cocked for the wild dogs, but everything remained peaceful. Now and then a cricket chirped, and in the distance a whippoorwill cooed. A dozen or so of her hens had escaped the slaughter of the night before and had begun to emerge hesitantly from their hiding places in the surrounding bush. She watched one hop onto the porch.

Rachel marveled once again at the unexpected neatness of her little homestead. The work crew had done far more than she had expected. The yard was pristine with no sign of last night's carnage. The huge screened front door had been repaired with good sturdy slats across the bottom half, and rehung. The slanting floor had been jacked up and wedges inserted to make it level. The loose arm on the swing had been nailed solidly and slats had been hammered across all the windows against the prowling of the dogs or other wild creatures so that she might leave them open at night to catch the breezes. She wished now that she had been home to thank the men and Slim for their efforts.

"I wish we still had a television." Pete climbed up on the log, straddling it to dangle his feet in the water.

"We'll get another soon," said Rachel.

"But I wish we had one now."

Rachel scooped up water, splashing it on her face, her arms. "I'll make a down payment on one with my very first paycheck. How's that?"

Pete wasn't in a mood to be pacified. "I think we'll always be poor!"

"No, we won't. That's one promise I'll make you, Pete. We're just going through a tough period. It'll make us strong, you'll see. Why don't you check your fish trap? And, while you're at it, move it closer. I don't want you to go around the bend out of sight in the future."

"You think the dogs'll come back?"

"No, but we want to be safe anyway."

Sara squealed. Rachel looked up, alarmed. Sara had been playing "Baby Moses on the Nile" and now Miss Mossy, lying on a short piece of old wood, was caught by the current and hurtling downstream. Rachel raced to retrieve the doll. "Maybe we'd better tie a string on your rafts so they won't get away from you again, pumpkin," Rachel told her youngest. But Sara was having none of it. She gathered up her wet dolls, put them in her buggy and set up house by a tree stump. Rachel laughed. So much for Moses. Sara wasn't trusting any of her babies to the creek again.

7

"THERE'S GRANDMA looking out the window!" exclaimed Caroline as her mother pulled up in front of the neat small house. "I'll bet she's baked cookies for us."

"Probably she has," agreed Rachel with false heartiness. *But only so she can complain how she slaved in a hot kitchen in the heat of summer*, she added silently. She gave the children a last inspection as they tumbled from the car. Untidy hair or ragged nails were sure to be remarked upon. "Pete, see if you can get your cowlick under control."

"Rachel! It's so good to see you," cooed Adele as she came through the front door, meaning not a word of it. "And you children," she added, only a little less insincerely. "My, how you've grown. Come along, come along . . . into the dining room, the kitchen's still a bit ovenish. I've baked your favorite," she said, beaming at Caroline. "Chocolate chip with nuts."

"Thank you, Grandma," Caroline said primly.

Smiling with aching composure, Rachel said, "How are you, Adele?"

"With this heat? Why, even the garden society hasn't been active. Such weather! But, of course, since . . . well, I haven't gone out too much. It wouldn't be seemly." She patted her already perfectly groomed gray hair with a stout hand.

The gesture was pure affectation, Rachel knew. "Clive's been dead for more than five months now, Adele. It would do you good to get back into the swing of things."

"Oh, I couldn't. What would people think? Oh my, Sara. What's that dirty thing you've got under your arm?"

"That's Miss Mossy, Grandma," explained Pete.

"Well, outside with it," she ordered dourly.

Sara hung on to Miss Mossy and hid behind Rachel's skirt.

"Really, Rachel, the thing is probably full of germs."

"She'll outgrow it soon enough."

"I don't suppose she's talking yet," Adele ventured with disapproval.

Rachel stiffened. "Not yet."

"You should take her to another specialist."

"And what would I pay him with?"

Adele's eyes glittered. "If Clive had only—only lived, I'm sure he would have provided well for the children. Death is so unexpected."

"Especially Clive's." Rachel regretted the sarcasm the moment it left her tongue. "We shouldn't be discussing this in front of the children," she amended.

The old lady's chin nodded. Her petulant mouth drooped.

"You can't keep them in a fairy-tale world forever, Rachel. It's not healthy. I want my grandchildren to know things, to excel."

Like you wanted your own son to excel, thought Rachel with a measure of impatience. Why was it only now, after he was dead, she wondered, that she was coming to know Clive, coming to understand what drove him, coming to know why he was never satis-

fied? In a burst of understanding she realized it wasn't
her that Clive couldn't face after he had been arrested.
It was his mother. In that moment the layers of guilt
over Clive's dying began to fall away.

"Some wild dogs killed my pig, Grandma. Sheriff
Stark—"

Adele's hand fluttered at her throat. "So it's true,
then!" Her tone was thick with accusation as she turned
on Rachel. "I heard you've been seeing that horrible
man. I just didn't want to believe it."

"I haven't been seeing him, Adele. Not in the way you
mean. Garrett has been helpful. A wild animal killed
Pete's pig and—"

"Oh, it's Garrett, now, and my son not even cold in
his grave."

Rachel clenched her hands until her nails bit deep into
the flesh of her palms. Caroline began to whimper.
"Mama, is Daddy cold?"

"Adele—" Rachel said, then shook her head in
disbelief. "Listen, maybe I'd better take the children
along with me."

"No, no, you don't have to do that. I only meant that
you don't have time for self-indulgence, Rachel. Stop
crying, Caroline, you're making me nervous."

Rachel gathered Caroline into her arms. "Listen,
darling, your daddy's in heaven. It's nice and warm
there. He's happy now. Grandma was just using a figure of speech." She gave the older woman a withering
look as she ushered her small brood outside. "We'll be
going now. It was nice seeing you, Adele."

"You can't keep me from my grandchildren. That's
what you're trying to do."

"Come out to the house anytime, Adele," Rachel
answered, forcing a pleasant tone until the children had

shuffled ahead. Then she turned on the older woman, her anger flaring. "I won't let you do to my children what you did to Clive. I won't! I won't have you frightening them or making them feel like second-class citizens."

"You were wrong for Clive. If I told him once, I told him a thousand times. If he hadn't married you, he'd be alive today."

Rachel gave her a pitying look. "I don't think so, Adele. And you know what? I'm glad we had this—this set-to today. It's opened my eyes."

"I didn't mean... But one must endure, mustn't one?"

Rachel's anger toward her mother-in-law was tempered by the persistent notion that the pompous old woman was just as scared of the future as she herself was. She said goodbye with a trace more charity than the situation warranted. "Another time, Adele..."

In the car, Rachel shivered violently, although it was stifling hot. She had a sudden morbid vision of what her future was to be. Unloved, no man in her life, no father for her children, no loving parents to help soften the loneliness. That was what being a widow was all about.

IN HIS OFFICE, Garrett pounded on the ancient air conditioner with his fist and gave a satisfied sigh when cool air shot out of the vents.

"She's really a looker, ain't she?"

Garrett spun around and stared at Slim Walters. The deputy had a penchant for gossip and was too often indiscreet. "Who's a looker?"

"The Cameron woman. 'Course when I knew her, she was the skinny Wallis kid. Couldn't call her skinny no more. No, sir. Not skinny." He guffawed and canted a sly look at his boss.

When Garrett was very angry, his lips compressed in a single thin white line, the thick dark eyebrows seemed to meet above his snapping blue eyes and the muscles in his neck went rigid.

"Do you like working for me, Walters?" he asked in a flat passionless voice that did not betray his fury.

"Sure I do. You—"

"Then get up off your duff and get on patrol. And while you're at it, check with every farmer and rancher in the south end of the county to see if those wild dogs have been on the prowl again."

"Check with... I can do that by phone. Besides, I got these daily reports to finish from last week."

"I don't really care if you've got daily reports from the last thousand years. Get out of my sight. Now!"

Slim pushed back his chair from the desk and lumbered to his feet. "Hey, man, I'm goin'. I'm goin'. But tell me, why're you pickin' on me?"

Slim didn't expect an answer and he didn't get one. Garrett had already put the deputy out of his mind. Rachel was lodged there now, and Rachel was to blame for his unruly passions. He had a picture in his mind. Rachel in bed, his bed, one arm stretched over the pillow, her chestnut hair flowing outward soft and fragrant, and he was watching the enticing rise and fall of her breasts, her shapely legs and, between them, the lure that made him go bone hard. He couldn't sleep, he couldn't eat and he couldn't seem to open his mouth without jumping down somebody's gullet.

He was furious with himself. Hell, he was an out-and-out coward. He had become obsessed by a sexual fantasy—and every time he got near Rachel he backed off, fearful that he couldn't make the fantasy real. There was nothing, no one, so doomed as a timid lover. He'd have to make up his mind to do something soon, if only to rid himself of the damnable ache in his loins. An ache that was building, growing within and striving to be unleashed. *Hell*, he thought, grabbing his old felt hat off the rack, *what am I standing around here for?*

IF THE ABORTED VISIT to Adele's had left Rachel and the children subdued, Rachel was also suffering vague distaste at having had to request Clive's death certificate for a second time. She wanted desperately to be finished with death. And Clive. She had loved him, he was the father of her children—these were facts not to be disputed, but now . . . now she did not want to look back. Memories, good or bad, were just that—memories. She could not take succor from them. The future loomed, engulfing her day by day. That was where she wanted to be, looking forward.

To lift the children's spirits she had taken them for a walk along the upper reaches of the creek, pointing out muskrat huts and tree stumps that beavers had gnawed. After they had startled a covey of quail into flight, there had come a sudden quiet, and fright had overtaken her. She remembered the wild dogs and so their walk had been aborted. Now they were lazing the afternoon away, she in the swing, Caroline reading on the stoop, Sara engrossed with her dolls and Pete trying to entice them into going swimming.

Caroline let loose an exuberant sigh, a prelude to her seemingly innocuous question. "Is Grandma going to stay mad at us forever, Mama?"

With a sinking feeling Rachel realized all her efforts had only postponed this discussion. "Of course not.

She just wasn't in the best of moods today. It's the heat. I'll write her a note asking her to lunch next week. She'll come. She loves you."

"Do you like Grandma?" Caroline's big round eyes were all innocence.

Rachel smiled weakly. "A wife has to like her mother-in-law, no matter how much she doesn't. Remember that."

"You're not making sense, Mama."

"Yes, I am. You'll see."

"Anyway, I don't think Grandma loves you."

"All mothers feel that way toward their son's wives at first."

"You mean when I get married, you won't like my wife?" asked Pete.

Rachel laughed and some of the dark gloom she'd been suffering melted away. "Pete, darling," she said, eyeing the wet towel he'd dropped on the stoop, his shoes and socks scattered in the yard, his shirt hanging over the porch railing, "if you will only marry a girl who will pick up after you, I promise to adore her."

"It's not going to be anytime soon, y'know. I'm still only nine."

"In that case, gather up your things and put them where they belong. And get out of those dripping shorts."

He looked longingly at the rippling creek. "I'd like another swim."

"Not today. I thought we'd plan a party." Rachel watched the two young faces and knew she'd hit on just the thing to erase from their minds the scene at Adele's that morning.

"It's not anybody's birthday," declared Caroline, her voice deliberately devoid of expression to cover her excitement. But Rachel could tell, could see Caroline's shoulder jerk, her stomach going in and out.

"It doesn't have to be. Each of you can invite one friend for a week from Saturday. I'll bake a cake and you can cook hot dogs and marshmallows—"

"Billy Evans for me!" said Pete, grinning.

"Janice Sizemore, then," said Caroline, looking unconcerned.

"And who for Sara?" asked Rachel, watching the child draw a playhouse in the dirt beneath the mulberry tree.

"Billy's little sister? She was always trying to tag along after me and Billy when we lived in town."

"I think so," agreed his mother. "We'll ask them when we go to church next Sunday."

Pete's face got quiet, thoughtful. "I knew there'd be a catch."

Sara came running up to the porch, her little legs pumping hard, and in the next instant a car rounded the switchback and came to a halt beneath the mulberry tree. Rachel stood up, trying to steady the violent beating of her heart while Sara sat on the steps and whimpered.

Before Garrett could emerge from his car, Rachel ordered him to move it back a length.

"You're not getting rid of me that easily this time," he called.

Rachel stepped off the porch. "You've driven over Sara's playhouse. She drew one in the dirt."

"Oh." He moved the car and when he did, Rachel saw he had a passenger. A woman. His mother! Rachel had a nodding acquaintance with Mrs. Stark. Enough to say hello when their paths crossed in the grocer's or the post office, but she'd never actually held a conversation with the lean pleasant-faced woman who wore her white hair plaited in a coil around her head. She looked from Garrett to his mother, marshaling her wits, but unable to hide her puzzlement.

"Something tells me that you weren't expecting us, Rachel," Mrs. Stark said by way of greeting. She darted a look at her son. His bold features hinted at humor but he said nothing, so she smiled down at Sara. "My, I haven't seen you since you were a wee thing."

Rachel answered, "I wasn't, Mrs. Stark, but please make yourself at home. Sit in the swing. Pete, Caroline, introduce yourselves to Mrs. Stark." Rachel dropped her smile and her voice as she turned to Garrett. "I just know you have an explanation."

"I do. Let's walk down to the creek, shall we?" He took her arm, propelling her forcefully toward the twisting path through emerald shadows.

"If I don't, you'll drag me."

"Be nice, Rachel. I'm here to take you to dinner. And if I want to take you to dinner, you have to have a baby-sitter. I've thought of everything, you see."

Rachel gaped, trying to fix his words in her mind. Trying to make sense of them while wild spurts of excitement warmed her flesh. Garrett laughed at her response. *A coup, by damn!* he exulted. He put a finger beneath her chin and gently closed her mouth.

His touch brought Rachel to her senses. "Your gall is beyond conceit! I'm not going anywhere with you." Oh, but she wanted to. To be out for an evening in an adult world. A sane world. Dinner, with music, a wonderfully thick steak, people waiting on her. There wasn't any reason why she shouldn't agree, except . . . except that she was drawn so to Garrett. And it was his neg-

ligence... She didn't want to think about that now. She
had been alone so long. Too long.

"Don't be so hasty," cautioned Garrett, seeing her
expression waver. A little smile lifted the corners of his
mouth.

"I'm not leaving my kids with a stranger while I
go—"

"Take a look back over your shoulder. Don't you
think they'd be safe and content with Mom?"

Forced to look because his splayed hand was putting
pressure on the small of her back in such a familiar way,
setting her flesh on fire beneath the thin shirt, Rachel
noted that Caroline and Pete held places on either side
of Mrs. Stark in the swing. And Sara. Sara, grinning,
was in the woman's lap while Mrs. Stark was whispering some foolishness in the tiny shell of her ear. Rachel
felt a twinge of jealousy. She didn't like another woman
usurping her place in her children's lives. And after all
she'd done for her offspring, there they were, being
disloyal. It was an unreasonable thought, unfair to the
children. But the jealousy stayed, tightening her resis-
tance.

"So?" Her voice was hardly more than the chirp of a
sparrow.

"So, go get dressed."

"Garrett, I'm not going out with you. That would be
a date. I haven't had a date in almost twelve years."

"You're worried about how to act."

Rachel put her hands over her eyes. "You're beyond
belief." And so were her tempest-stricken nerves. She
could almost pick out every vein in her body, so hot,
so furious did her blood course through them.

"Rachel." His voice was unaccountably soft. "Here's
the way it is. If you aren't dressed and ready to go in

twenty minutes, I'm afraid that I'll just have to report that illegal fish trap parked in White Hawk Creek practically on your doorstep."

"That's Pete's. You wouldn't!"

He shrugged his powerful shoulders. "It's my duty. The fish and game department stocks the pond that feeds that creek with fish to draw the tourists. Fly-fishing's all that's legal. Fines are outrageous, I hear."

"You're doing it again, Garrett. Making threats. Is that the only way you can get a woman to go out with you? What happened to all that charm I used to hear so much about?"

"Charm doesn't seem to work on you."

"You're so right." She pivoted and began angling up the path.

Garrett watched. Her head was held too high, her spine straight as a newly planed board. It wasn't the carriage of a woman going to get dressed for a date. Rachel was trying to outmaneuver him. She was heading for the porch and would probably just sit there, talking, until it was too late to go anywhere. She was being selfish. And he hadn't even smoked a cigar, just to keep his breath sweet tasting.

He admired steely integrity, admired loyalty, admired guts, admired brains, but damn it, he admired it best in a man. Women . . . well, women were bone and muscle and blood and lush and were supposed to fall all over him. Rachel Cameron wasn't falling. She was still as upright as a preacher's wife. He had to pull out all the stops. With just the right amount of soft chagrin, he said, "You wouldn't embarrass me in front of my mother, would you, Rachel?"

Her step faltered and she turned to look at him. The late afternoon sun cast a shimmering glow upon his

windburned features. A breeze, scooping coolness from
the surface of the creek, ruffled his black hair and, hat
in hand, he was beating an impatient tattoo against a
lean thigh. For an instant he appeared as vulnerable as
she, but that was impossible. He was Garrett Stark and
Lackawanna County was his kingdom. Embarrass
him? *Yes!* But common sense failed to overrule what
was in her heart.

"I guess not," she said, capitulating.

"RACHEL, DEAR." Mrs. Stark was unleashing a modi-
cum of exasperation into the hamburger patties she was
shaping. "You've shown me where the children's night-
clothes are twice, pointed out the bathroom on the side
porch, and warned me about Pete's pranks, Caroline's
haughtiness, Sara's silences, who likes ketchup and who
doesn't. Pointed out aspirin, salves, and which tooth-
brush belongs to whom. I think I can manage. After all,
you're only going to be gone for a year—"

"Oh, no, only—"

"Just so you won't worry overmuch," continued Mrs.
Stark, talking fast, "I know how to set bones, suck a
snakebite and sew up a flap of skin, too."

Rachel dropped her arms, smiling sheepishly. "I'm
that bad?"

"I'd give you the prize."

Rachel met the older woman's eyes, saw the laughter
there. "But I hate for you to have to cook. Leave the
dishes. This is all so unexpected. I'd die if the children
misbehaved. Besides that, it's awkward to have a man
ask you out in one breath and produce his mother to
baby-sit in the next!"

Martha Stark laughed. "Garrett can be very persua-
sive when he's of a mind to be. Now, don't you worry

about the kiddies. I raised Garrett and lived through it. I'll manage your three, who're far more mannerly than Garrett was at their age, believe me."

"Was Garrett bad when he was a little boy?"

"When he ran away to join the Marines I cried my heart out. All my friends thought I was heartbroken. I was crying from relief. He's mellowed some, thank goodness."

"What about your husband, Garrett's dad?"

"Killed in the Korean conflict."

"Oh, I'm sorry. I never heard."

"Well, we widows have to stick together now, don't we? Look at it this way, dear, we're just trading children for an evening. And I think I like yours better."

Rachel decided she liked Mrs. Stark. "I hope you won't be offended, but I think I like mine better, too."

"It's no wonder, none of them smoke smelly old cigars."

"But I like—" Rachel's face flamed. "I think I'll go into the bathroom to put my hair up. There's more light there."

"Yes, do that," agreed Martha Stark. She tilted her head to look out the front window at Garrett, pacing to-and-fro on the porch. "He's getting impatient."

8

As Garrett ushered Rachel into his car he considered himself a happy man. He positioned his hat carefully on the seat between them and looked to see if she had noticed. But Rachel's eyes kept darting anxiously toward the group standing on the porch waving goodbye. Rachel looked pretty, but was dressed too primly for his taste in a neat coral-colored suit. She had buttoned the jacket so that only the bow-tied jabot of her white cotton blouse poked out. Her hair was in a lustrous mass atop her head, and in the heat, loose tendrils were already damp and clinging to her neck. The way she was dressed, it was as if she were daring him.

Daring him to do what? Pick a fight probably. He started the engine and out of habit reached toward the air conditioner, but instead of turning it on, he flexed his hand. "Air conditioner's on the blink," he said. "You can roll the window down."

"No, the wind would mess my hair."

"Suit yourself."

By the time they had reached the highway and turned north the inside of the car had become stifling. Inside of another mile, Rachel's suit jacket was folded over her lap like a wilted flag of truce and her blouse was untied and unbuttoned down to her tanned cleavage. She checked her hair in an unconsciously feminine gesture. It brought her full breasts into sharp relief and caused a reaction in Garrett he tried to suppress. She smoothed the coral fabric in her lap. "I can put it back on when we get to the restaurant."

"Glad to see you loosen up." He sounded hoarse to his own ears and cleared his throat. The scent she wore filled the close confines of the car. *Roses,* Garrett thought. He sniffed, knowing he should say something nice about it, get her to relax. "You . . . you sure do smell," he declared, watching her out of the corner of his eye.

"I what?" Rachel rasped, swallowing the words.

"I can smell you—"

She fumed with anger. "Do you think that's nice? Saying I *smell*. I'm wearing perfume."

Garrett felt his mood of hopefulness fading. "Well, damn! I didn't say you stink, did I?"

"You're so unromantic, I can't imagine what women see in you." She turned to look out the window, staring at the scenery, seeing it and not seeing it.

Garrett was crushed. "What did you want me to say? Something sissy like, 'Gee, what's that perfume you're wearing? It makes my senses swim, yum, yum.'"

"Nobody's asking you to be a sissy! Or sarcastic. You could be thoughtful, but no, not Sheriff Stark." She didn't look at him and she didn't plan to.

"What is that supposed to mean?" He rolled down his window a crack, drinking in the waft of breeze it afforded.

"Only that you know this is the first time I've been out with a man in years. You could have made . . . it should be special."

He was quiet for a moment. "Would flowers make it special?"

"Flowers?"

"From the florist in Hickory Grove."

"No one's given me flowers since my high school prom." She sounded wistful. "Not even—"

"On the seat, under my hat," Garrett told her, not daring to glance at her but imagining the look on her face. He waited for her to say something. And waited. *She's too overcome with emotion*, he thought. "Well?"

"You're sitting on them."

Muttering a vile string of expletives, he wound the window all the way down, lifted his hip and yanked the crushed bouquet from beneath him and tossed it out the window. "How's that for being romantic!"

Rachel caught a flash of yellow. "Stop!" she yelled.

Garrett slowed, pulled over to the shoulder. "All right, get it out of your system. Tell me what an animal I am, lay it on. I'm venal, I'm immoral, I'm cruel. Well, go on, say it. You want to, I can hear your teeth grinding." He was glaring at her so hard his eyes were flat. He yanked his hat out of her hand and jammed it on his head, snapping the brim.

Rachel glared right back. "Those were my flowers," she said with infinite calm. "Turn around and go get them."

"But they're—"

She folded her arms over her heaving breasts, and stared straight out in front of her like a stone sphinx. "You had no right to throw them away."

"I knew you wanted to start a fight. I knew it the minute you stepped out of the house leading with your chin and that damned blouse tied up to your gullet with that jacket wrapped around you like armor. Yes, ma'am, I knew it!" He slapped the steering column with the palm of his hand, then yanked a cigar out of his shirt. When he had it lit and the car filled with blue smoke, Rachel lowered her window. "Roll it up," he ordered and flipped on the air conditioner.

Jets of frosty air burst over them. Rachel bristled. "Not only are you an Indian giver, but you're a liar, too."

"Oh, I'm so many things, you just don't know." His scorn was as thick as the smoke unfurling from his cigar. The motor hummed. A car went past, heading south. The driver lifted his hand, Garrett answered the salute, raising his cigar.

"I was thinking, Garrett," said Rachel slowly, "that after dinner I would let you kiss me."

A kiss! he thought, burning with malevolence. A thousand kisses wouldn't satisfy the craving that was eating at him. He opened his mouth to tell her, and closed it. Adrenaline began to spurt and flow.

"All this fun," he said, groaning laconically, "and the evening is hardly begun." He swung the car around in a U-turn, squealed to a stop in the middle of the highway, opened his door and scooped up...shredded green paper and mostly flowerless stems. "Guess that car..." He sorted through the mess, finding one bent stem with a dangling bloom. He handed it to her. "Started out being yellow rosebuds," he said.

"Thank you," she said.

They drove some miles in silence, into Hickory Grove, past Nester's Café, past Lu Chin's, the Chinese restaurant, past the lumber mill, out of Hickory Grove. Surprised, Rachel turned in her seat and stared out the back window.

"Don't say a word," warned Garrett.

"No, of course not," she agreed and lifted the broken stem to her nose. The rest of the petals fell off. She smiled inwardly, gathered them up and put them in her purse.

When he turned off the highway onto a narrow lane that had brush and even small trees growing between twin paths, she said, "You don't expect me to keep quiet now, do you?"

His glance at her was brief, taking in her demurely fixed mouth, the thickly lashed gray-green eyes that were beginning to smolder once again. "Didn't expect to get you past Hickory Grove without an argument. Sure don't now."

"I'm not going to argue. But you can't tell me there's a restaurant at the top of this mountain." They were going steadily higher, the ill-kept path curving ever upward. Pine, poplar and ash leaned into the roadway, brushing against fenders and windows as they moved past.

"I said I was taking you to dinner. I didn't name the place."

"Do you mind naming it now?" she asked icily.

"You'll know soon enough. Get off your high horse." His hands were gripping the wheel hard and she could see the bones running from his wrists to his fingers. His hands had figured often in her thoughts. And those thoughts had led to pulsating erotic sensations. Rachel's stomach began to flutter with uncommon activity.

The path came to an end under the shady canopy of an incredibly old oak that was shedding its gray rough bark. Gnarled roots spread out every which way, clutching at the soil. A small cabin, as solid-looking as the old tree, crouched beneath its heavy limbs.

Rachel stared at Garrett and Garrett stared at her. He exhaled slowly. "We're here," he said, and seeing the storm building in her expression, moved like a whip out of the car and around to her door, opening it with a flourish to hand her out.

A slow wind, heavy with the breath of summer leaves and hidden violets, ruffled her hair. "What I had thought," Rachel said, her voice strained, "was that we were going to a place with waiters, and music, and people."

"People!" uttered Garrett in genuine astonishment. "You're always surrounded by people. I want us to be alone."

Rachel's chin went up a degree. "Alone?"

He nodded, taking a better grip on his cigar with his teeth. "I figured the reason we didn't . . . you wouldn't . . . the other night was because we weren't alone. So..." He leaned against the car, folding his arms against his chest. He had to, otherwise he'd reach for her, touch her, and it was too soon. Everything had to be just right.

Not even a dim light was necessary to illuminate what Garrett had in mind, what he had planned down to the tiniest detail. She was staggered. "Did it ever occur to you," she choked, "did it ever . . . did you stop to think that you caught me at a very vulnerable moment before? That I might have refused at the last . . ." She closed her eyes. "Oh, dear God . . ."

"You're not upset, are you?"

I'm an adult. I can handle this, Rachel thought. "No, not at all," she said sweetly, and Garrett's smile was wonderful to behold.

"Well! Well, then. First, we eat . . ." He began removing things from the trunk of the car. A folding grill, charcoal, an ice chest, a tablecloth, a fat candle that had gone soft and sagged in the heat. He stared at it for a moment in dismay, tossing it back, then dragged out canvas folding chairs, one of which he yanked open and put solidly near the single step that led into the cabin. "You sit right here," he ordered, "while I broil us a mean steak. I've got wine. You like wine, don't you?"

Rachel collapsed into the chair. "I just love wine. You've thought of everything, haven't you?"

He stood before her, khakis crisp, eyes shaded by his hat brim, cigar dead in his mouth, hands on his hips. He might have caught just a touch of scorn in her voice, but no, her features were calm, lovely to look at. He felt his mouth going suddenly dry. "I tried," he admitted modestly.

First, we eat, Rachel thought. *And second?* She folded her hands in her lap. A prim ladylike gesture. But all she wanted to do was stop their trembling.

A gentle stillness descended on the high mountain as the sun moved toward the far western horizon. The wide screened door of the cabin had cotton balls stuffed in rips to keep out insects. Garrett went in and out of the cabin to retrieve cutlery and a folding table over which he positioned the cloth. He had refused her offer of help and she was content not to help him, lest dinner come and go before she had things straight in her mind.

"Who did you borrow this place from?" she asked, thinking of the gossip it would cause and her pending application before the school board.

"No one. It's mine. A quarter of the mountain, too. My dad left it to me. We used to come up here a lot— when I was little, of course." He shot her a sly glance. "I was conceived up here."

Rachel took a quick sip of her wine. "Is that right?"

"Mom says so."

"I thought you lived with her."

"In a room over the garage, not the house. This is my . . . place. Used to dream about it when I was in the Marines."

"Do you bring other . . . other people up here?"

"You mean women?" He stirred the coals in the grill. They were beginning to glow, forming a layer of ash.

"I mean anybody!"

"Don't get snappish. Your food won't set right, you'll get indigestion."

Rachel didn't think she'd have to worry about indigestion. Nothing would reach her stomach. It couldn't. Swallowing was beyond her.

"I don't bring anyone up here. Mom comes once in a great while. When she's feeling moody. That's all."

"Then why me?"

"We needed a place. Privacy."

She wanted to scream at him. Tell him she wouldn't do what he was thinking. What she was thinking. She couldn't. She had a stretch mark. She couldn't, wouldn't let a man see that. She was going to remain celibate the rest of her life. It just made her feel good to have a man flirting with her. Looking at her with approval the way Garrett had, the way he was looking now.

He slapped the steaks on the grill, began slicing tomatoes. "Snitched these from your garden while you were getting dressed. Hope you don't mind."

"No." Tell him now, she ordered herself. Tell him now! "Garrett . . ."

Dusk rose around them, deepening shadows threw the oak, the cabin, Garrett's lean body into dark relief, and the sky gleamed with blue and purple streaks of light. He went into the cabin for a kerosene lantern.

When he had it glowing and the wick adjusted, he looked at her, "You were saying?"

"I—I never did thank you for having my place cleaned up."

"No trouble. The men were happy to see blue sky. Slim said you didn't want the carcass?"

"No."

"He brought back a rib and the ham. Jail cook barbecued it for the men."

"I'm glad. I hated to see it wasted, but we just couldn't. Pete raised it from a baby."

The sun set behind the ragged edge of the mountain, stars flew up into the dark sky like fireflies. A nighthawk fluttered its wings, swooping overhead, and seemed to skid in the air as if confused or startled to find two human beings in his hunting grounds. Garrett called Rachel to the table. She went. *He's gone to so much trouble*, she thought. *It's only this one time. Never again.* In the soft glow of the kerosene lantern her face was pale, as if sculpted from chalk.

She carved her steak into about a hundred pieces, making little mounds of it with the tomatoes and cold asparagus. Eating it was out of the question for her stomach was stretching this way and that in queasy undulations.

Tobacco smoke drifted in the air. It was a man smell, vital. She glanced up, discovering Garrett staring at her, his light-colored eyes glacial in the lantern light. He was leaning forward, his elbows propped on the small table. His hair gleamed blue-black. "I think I'd like a smoke, too," she said, reaching for her purse.

He struck a match, lighting it for her. "All right. Talk me out of it. Or yourself."

She inhaled deeply. "It doesn't seem right, not with you being the one—"

"Who let Clive Cameron die," he finished, his voice as hard as forged steel. "Bury him, Rachel, but don't bury him between us. You loved him? I envy him that. He had an odd twist in his makeup. You had to know that. He liked to deceive, he thrived on it. You were part of the deceit. When the curtain went up on his game, he couldn't face it. Or maybe it was his mother he didn't want to face. This is a small county. I've heard the stories, and the excuses of why good old Clive wasn't president of the bank or the rotary. His tail was in a crack, and he took . . . he took the wrong way out. Because he couldn't blame anyone else for his getting caught. And I did catch him, Rachel. Red-handed. Hauling speakers out of a car."

"That's not true." But it was. She knew it. She didn't want to hear it put into words. "You think I'm going to sit here and listen to this? You're maligning the dead! That's reprehensible."

"It's fact. That's what my job is all about—facts. Clive seldom worked. Didn't you once ever wonder where his money came from?"

Rachel didn't answer at once. She was shocked at Garrett, at herself, because part of her was listening, and agreeing. "There was never all that much extra above his unemployment checks and when they ran out . . . just odd jobs," she whispered.

Garrett wanted only to grab her up, take her in to the bed he had prepared inside the cabin and lose himself inside her. But this purging had to be done. Clive Cameron's ghost had to be put to rest. "The odd jobs were stealing."

She toyed with her cigarette, refusing to look at him. "You think you know a person because conversations interrupted by children, by the telephone, or by a visit to the doctor are easy to resume however long the intervals. You think you're on the same wavelength, you . . ." And then she looked up at Garrett. His eyes were clear, his features strong, and he was smiling at her, offering her the strength she could no longer get from Clive's memory or find within herself. She laughed, a small thin sound tinged with irony. "You're the only man I've ever met that manages to get me into a corner one way or another," she told him.

"What about the corner you're in now?" he asked, and held his breath.

"I'm not sure." The words were as frail as the ash that fell away from her cigarette.

"But you've had a bit of time for yourself, some peace and quiet?"

"I don't get that in your company."

"You can, if that's all you want—or need."

She looked at him with a quick sharp upward tilt of her chin. "Don't go taking my needs upon yourself. Just don't!"

"But I am, Rachel. I don't give up, or in, easily."

Outside the small circle of light, the mountain hummed with life. Night creatures buzzed, slithered, fluttered, chirped, hooted, calling to one another, calling . . . mating. "What is it that you want, then?" Her voice was shaking.

"You know that already. You."

There came a sudden scurrying and then the quick silence of small creatures going into the ground, and the stars seemed to burn cold and blue and close. Rachel heard herself speaking, shouting she thought, though her voice was so faint Garrett leaned forward to hear. "I want you, too," she said.

ONCE INSIDE THE CABIN with its thick-timbered ceiling and washed-pine walls, such an awkwardness descended upon them both that Rachel didn't know whether to laugh or cry. The uppermost question in her mind was: who was going to undress first. To cover her hesitation she made a pretense of exploring the one room. All she had to do was pivot slowly.

The bed was a wide old-fashioned four-poster with plump pillows and a thin quilt that was pulled drum tight, military fashion. Above the bed a wide window had been opened to let in a breeze and the first faint sliver of moonlight. Along one wall, built flush to an ancient cookstove, was a wooden counter upon which sat a jug of water, a washbasin and the kerosene lantern, its wick now turned very low. Winter and summer clothing drooped from wall pegs. Two dowdy, comfortable-looking chairs held court before a narrow-mouthed stone chimney. Lamplight did not carry to the corners, but Rachel could pick out a broomstick, boots, a lopsided stack of adventure magazines. Her eyes roved quickly past Garrett, arms folded, leaning tall and powerful against the doorjamb. He was openly, unashamedly, hungrily staring. Rachel felt faint. Garrett cleared his throat.

"I'd go outside while you undress, except I've been thinking of this moment for so long...."

"Turn out the lamp, then." It was a plea.

"No."

It seemed to Rachel that he almost floated as he closed the space between them. "You're not thinking about daring the devil, are you, Rachel?"

"I don't know what you mean."

He fingered the trailing jabot. The back of his hand lightly brushed her breasts. Beneath the soft clinging cotton they began to hum and swell. "What I mean is, you're not planning on backing out, not when we've come this far?" He moved his hands to her waist, and she felt the weight of bone, the breadth of his hand span in the firm pressure he exerted. "Put your arms around me, Rachel."

She did, glorying in the hard feel of him as her small hands traveled, palms flat, to meet at his spine. The tiniest whoosh of air escaped her throat. She thought, *I'm not going to survive this.*

He held her gently, yet where their bodies touched she could feel tendon and sinew growing taut. His. Hers. Until instinctively, she pressed her face into his shoulder. Reveling in the feel of his muscled chest against her breasts, Rachel's arms tightened about him. And then his arms were about her, too, an impregnable shelter, a haven from which she had no desire to flee.

Garrett's mouth urgently sought hers and Rachel succumbed to the treacherous leap of her pulse. His warm lips moved with a racking hunger, his tongue searched entry, found it and thrust deep. Hot blood roared into his manhood; swollen, it throbbed against her abdomen. *Oh, I'm lost,* she thought, for she had no defense against the potent magic he wreaked upon her senses. And then the truth: she wanted no defense, she wanted him with all her heart.

His lips never leaving hers, Garrett swept her up in his arms and carried her to the bed. He laid her down gently. Then, oddly shy, he sat on the bed, his back to her, and began to remove his clothes. Right boot, left boot, belt, khaki shirt, undershirt. He moved off the bed then, to put these items neatly on the back of one of the chairs.

Rachel watched him. She had to. His shoulders were broad, the arms revealing their well-honed muscles with every movement he made. His chest was matted with fine dark hair peppered with gray. His stomach was lean and a mean-looking scar accompanied the line of black hair disappearing tantalizingly into the worn khaki slacks. She would ask him about the scar later. Not now. Oh, not now, for he had discarded his pants and was returning to the bed where she lay, led to her, it seemed, by his rigid maleness jutting fiercely from the tangle of thick black curling hair.

"Want me to undress you?" asked Garrett as he lay down, resting his body lightly on hers. He began to nibble on her earlobe.

Rachel found her mouth too dry for speech, found herself light-headed, discovered her fingers trembling and clumsy in the small space between their bodies. "You'll have to move," she said huskily.

He didn't go far, only sliding off her enough so that his hands could follow hers, to peel her blouse back, to lower the straps of her undergarments, to undo hooks and zippers until her breasts thrust free, and she was wholly revealed, lithe, tanned and silky.

Garrett expelled a soft moan as his gaze drifted hungrily over Rachel's naked form. The breasts were round and white, thrust high. The nipples were large, tumescent, a lovely pink. Rachel's belly was firm and flat, falling down to the silkiness of the chestnut triangle of hair. Garrett's gaze lingered on that triangle for a long interval, then traveled down the long tanned legs. He cupped the white flesh of her breasts, his fingers moving to-and-fro over the erect nipples, and when he felt a rapid heavy trembling move through her entire body, he lifted his eyes, meeting Rachel's heavily lashed look for an instant. He dropped his head and touched his lips to the hardened nipples. His tongue made a liquid swirling motion across their tautness. Rachel moaned when his hand trailed up her thigh and his fingers danced lightly in her silken triangle.

A tiny fragment of her mind brought forth a fleeing moment of reality, and her own hand raced to put a stop to what Garrett was doing. Yet even as she attempted to brush his hand away, her hips undulated, reaching, arching with a passionate willful rhythm to meet his hand. A fiery ache of anticipation spread throughout her body. She wanted the pleasure she was feeling to last forever. . . . He fondled her breasts, sucked her nipples and Rachel watched him devour her.

Hungering to give Garrett pleasure, she caressed his shoulder, his chest, weaving her fingers through his hair, letting her hand fall, glide, drift until she took his great throbbing in her fingers, exploring it gently, tracing patterns of nothingness upon it, feeling it grow wild. Garrett gave a low ragged cry of pleasure and feverishly brought his hot moist mouth to hers. He shifted on the bed as if taking an instinctive measure of their bodies. Rachel felt his hardness pulsating, an engorged marauder—unerringly finding what it sought. She cried out, digging her fingers into his back. Her legs parted and Garrett thrust into her, and she arched her hips in ancient welcome of unendurable delight.

Each thrust was an exquisite agony releasing hot and angry emotions that clawed their way through her body; a liquid fire flowing and coursing through her veins, swelling them, conquering forever the passion she had held in check for so long.

Garrett felt the change within her. He murmured disconnected bits of love talk, coaxing Rachel to greater passion. Moving with a powerful incessant rocking motion he rose above her, feeling himself driving still deeper inside her. Impaling her, flesh against flesh.

He gave pleasure and took pleasure. He was aroused to a point he had never reached before. He had to bite back the spasms that racked him. Rachel was a sheath of wild hot silk enveloping the swollen rigid length of his shaft; a pulsating tormenting accommodating other self. Her pace quickened in erotic abandon, she locked her ankles at his waist and thrust her hips upward to receive him deeper. Gasping, he thought in a fleeting flare of recognition that she had ruined him for other women. No one but Rachel would do now. He tightened his muscles in control, losing it almost at once as she twisted beneath him, arching, tightening her legs so that his thrusts seemed unending and she accepted all of him. He was overwhelmingly conscious of her taut nipples brushing his chest, of the faint hint of roses, of the intimate way her body locked with his in a oneness that was shattering, unreal, savage.

Rachel felt the beginning of ecstasy, sensed the coming explosion. Primitive sensations began to resonate along nerve endings, causing a contracting and releasing of Garrett's incredibly swollen member. She expelled a triumphant shuddering tremolo, a cry of stunning pleasure. Her fingers bit into his shoulders, holding…holding until…the feeling. She lost all sense of time.

A driving fiery urgency made Garrett's head swim with need, a need that seemed to gouge out his insides, demanding he reach the pinnacle of release. And then the wonderful sensations grew in wild searing disorder, wave after wave exploding, erupting out of his loins.

It was silent in the cabin except for their ragged breathing. Rachel knew almost perfect contentment, without thought, without room for thought. "That was..." she began and stopped, for she couldn't think of words to describe what had just happened between them. It couldn't have been mere lust, could it? She was afraid to look at Garrett's face and find an answer sooner than she could bear to. She didn't know the rules. She felt awkward about the order of things. She wanted him to tell her, to whisper to her....

Garrett fell away from her, but kept an iron-tight arm around her waist and one leg resting across her thighs. "Magic," he said. "Except, I don't believe in magic. But it was different from..." His voice failed him. It was terrifying to be so taken with a woman. He could almost imagine being *married* to her! But even in his brain, the word had an unaccustomed sound. Marriage was likely the last thing he wanted. How he'd love to know what Rachel was thinking about right this minute. No! He wouldn't ask. He might make a fool of himself. Vanity was his curse. He breathed deeply. A dove cooed, the sound drifting in on the soft night air. "A penny for your thoughts...?" It was a safe innocuous question, one that could be answered in any way.

"I'm thinking... all the routines, the cooking, the washing, ironing, the children..."

Garrett's heart sank.

"I'm thinking about Clive and going through the motions of life. I'm thinking I've truly never made love before. I've been suffocating, dissolving in widowhood." The words were almost lost because she was speaking to herself rather than Garrett. Heart pounding, he rose up on an elbow to hear her better. "I never imagined that it could be like . . ." She tilted her head, gazing up at Garrett in the dim light, searching his face. "I've just been so lonely. It was lust, wasn't it?"

"I don't know." He suspected it wasn't, but a negative answer was too terrifying to contemplate. He was a bachelor through and through. Sex was just sex, he told himself. To Rachel, lying in his arms awaiting his reply, he said, "It went beyond the limit of anything I've ever experienced."

"Did it?"

"You don't object to my cigars, do you?"

She smiled up at him and drew a fingertip down the rugged planes of his face. "No, not at all. We have to be leaving soon, don't we?" She pressed her mouth to his throat, licking at it with the tip of her tongue.

"Not too soon," he said, and he was touching her in that special way, kissing her mouth, her cheek, her eyes...setting her breasts to quivering in a way that he found irresistible.

And Rachel thought that whatever happened—even if this was a once-in-a-lifetime experience—she'd never feel quite so alone again.

9

"DO I LOOK ALL RIGHT? My hair is fixed?" asked Rachel as she slid from the car and eyed her home anxiously.

"Anyone looking at you could tell you've been made love to twice over and then some," teased Garrett. "Especially my mother. She's got the eyes of a hawk."

"Don't make sick jokes."

With his hand on her elbow, Garrett paused and looked at her meaningfully. "Guilt sticks out all over you. We haven't done anything wrong. Stop thinking it. That's what shows."

"You're no help." Light poured onto the porch through the latched screened door. Rachel could see Mrs. Stark, head bowed on her chest, snoozing on the sofa. She opened her mouth to call softly and was stopped by Garrett placing a finger on her lips.

"Wait!" he whispered. "Are you happy?"

She studied him for a long moment, considering the question. *A very loaded question*, she thought. "I've never felt happier in my life," she replied lightly, "except when I graduated from college, and when Pete was born, and Caroline, and Sara. When I learned to drive, that made me happy—"

"Stop," he hissed, "or I'll be at the bottom of the heap."

"I didn't know you meant was I happy with you."

Their conversation, though low, woke his mother and she came to unlatch the screen. She smiled wearily.

"Were the children too much for you?" asked Rachel.

"I think I played too hard. I used to be terrific at jacks and charades. You two have a nice dinner?"

"It was lovely," said Rachel, and she meant it. "Thank you for coming out here and watching the children."

Martha Stark brushed this aside. She looked from Rachel to Garrett. "I invited the children to spend the night with me next Saturday. Pete said he would mow my lawn, Caroline and I are going to bake cookies and I promised Sara to make a dress for Miss Mossy." She shrugged, a helpless gesture. "I don't know how it came about, but I heard myself asking them."

"I do," answered Rachel with a small laugh. "You were manipulated. The little scamps are past masters at it. Don't worry. They'll forget."

"Oh, but I don't want them to forget. I'd like to have them. That is, if you don't mind."

Rachel's hand fluttered to her throat. "Oh, I don't know. They've never spent the night away from me. And what would I do with myself?"

"I could think of something," Garrett said lazily.

"I'm sure you could," was Rachel's withering reply. Then she blushed because Martha Stark was following their exchange with interest. "Mrs. Stark, it was wonderful of you to ask, but could I think about it and let you know?"

"Of course. However, you or Garrett would have to bring them. I don't drive, you know. And you could pick them up before church on Sunday."

"I'll decide before Saturday and be in touch."

"Yes." Mrs. Stark repinned a slipping wisp of braid. "Well, son, time to get me home."

As soon as his mother's back was turned, Garrett reached for Rachel.

"For heaven's sake!" Her voice lifted with an undercurrent of trepidation.

"For my sake," he drawled, taking her into his arms. His kiss was gentle, lingering. "Think about me," he said in parting.

"You mean, think about what a nice man you are, or how good you are in bed?"

Garrett put on a stern face. "Aren't I both?"

"You're just one thing—impossible. Now, take your mother home, like a good boy. It's late."

In the car, his mother asked, "How did the flowers go over?"

"Big. Real big," Garrett replied, and bit off the end of a cigar. "She was impressed."

"Don't light up one of those nasty things," ordered Martha with a mother's prerogative.

Garrett sighed heavily. "Yes, ma'am."

"WHY'D YOU HAVE TO GO OUT to eat last night? We have food here."

Rachel shook her head and sighed. "That's right, we do, but last night I didn't have to cook it."

Caroline twisted a strand of hair. "You could teach me how to cook, then when—"

"Darling, you're going to have to get used to the fact that now and again I want to be with adults. It doesn't mean I don't love you. I do, very much. Mothers need friends their own age, just as you children do."

"Are you going to let us spend the night with Mrs. Stark?"

"I said I'd think about it."

"We're going to bake cookies and have ice cream—"

"She's going to pay me two dollars to mow her lawn," put in Pete. "We need the money."

"Will both of you quit pestering me?" pleaded Rachel. "I said I'd think about it. And I will, if you'd just give me time."

Caroline eyed her mother slyly. "You always want time. Time means no. We have to wear you down first or you won't say yes. We'll get to watch television, too."

Sara leaned against her mother's knee and arranged a naked Miss Mossy in her lap. Rachel rolled her eyes heavenward. "All right, I'm feeling guilty. I'll let you go...provided you all help in the garden and keep your beds made. Now, if you don't mind, I've a letter to write—"

"Don't forget the invitations to the party. You promised."

"Caroline, my sweet daughter, you're pushing your luck."

The child grabbed her sister's hand. "C'mon, Sara, let's go find some roly-polies."

"Forget roly-polies. Pull weeds!" said Rachel to their retreating backs. "Independent little beasts!" she muttered after she was assured of a few moments of blessed silence. Taking pen and paper, she settled at the table, composing a letter to the school board to remind them that she was still waiting for a contract.

She couldn't get the letter right. Her thoughts kept shifting to Garrett and his name was the one she kept scribbling over the paper. Sheriff Stark. Garrett Stark. *Mrs. Garrett Stark.* Rachel Cameron Stark. Rachel Wallis Stark. She looked at the paper in amused disbelief. People didn't get married after going to bed together. Not nowadays, they didn't. She was dreaming.

She'd do best not to think about such things. She crumpled the paper.

She got angry—but not with Garrett, with herself. What a fool she was making of herself. Here she was building up a picture of the man that had no resemblance to him at all. She was just making him into what she wanted him to be. It was self-delusion.

Garrett had not mentioned a permanent relationship. He was just living up to his reputation.

He probably had women standing in line. The local stud, that's all he was. He was probably thinking that he had a live one, a widow starved for sex, the same as all men thought. And she had succumbed! She hated herself.

One thing: she wouldn't be so stupid again.

The most important thing in her life was the children. They were the only ones who really mattered. Saturday—he would be here Saturday. She was certain of that. She'd tell him . . . no more!

Pete stuck his head in the door. "Grandma's here!" He let the screen slam shut.

Rachel leaped from the table, flying about the house, picking up toys, spreading the linen over her bed, grabbing up breakfast dishes and stuffing them in the oven. The hurried activity was all for naught because Adele Cameron refused to go beyond the porch. "Well," said Rachel, pasting on a smile, "this is a pleasant surprise."

"Is it?" snorted the older woman. Rachel's spirits sank. So there was to be no smoothing over of their last argument.

Adele thrust a tin into Caroline's hands. "Here's the cookies you didn't get to have yesterday. Take them into the yard. I want to speak privately with your mother."

"Is it okay, Mama?"

Rachel nodded, then leaned against the porch railing and wrapped her arms tightly about herself. For a moment her eyes tracked the youngsters. She tried to separate her thoughts, to look at them coolly so that the flaring antagonism provoked by Adele would go away.

"It's all over town," the older woman said. "Everyone knows since the garden club met this morning. Martha Stark baby-sat while you went out with the sheriff. I don't understand you, Rachel. How could you?"

"I'm thirty-two years old, Adele, an adult—"

"You're selfish, disloyal and you've besmirched Clive's memory!"

"No, I haven't!" Rachel felt her eyes getting hot, threatening tears. She would not cry in front of Adele. She wouldn't give her that satisfaction.

"What will people think with you going around with the man who destroyed Clive's reputation?"

Quietly, as calmly as she could manage, Rachel said, "Clive ruined his own reputation. I didn't want to believe it, either. But he did. He stole things. That's how he supported us when he wasn't working."

"That's not true." Adele gasped, horrified.

"It is true! You don't want to see it. I don't blame you. I know it's hard."

"Hard?" The older woman's eyes narrowed to slits, her brow furrowed. "You don't know what hard is. Clive should never have married you. All you ever did was burden him. You and the children. A burden! You kept at my child, my only son, until he was a shell of his former self. You destroyed him! It was you. I'm the only person who ever understood him and you took him away from me."

Recoiling at the unjust vehemence directed toward her, Rachel studied her mother-in-law. No, former

mother-in-law. Now she knew what people meant
when they said a person was broken in spirit. Despite
Adele's carefully arranged hair, manicured nails and
neat dress, she sagged. Still, the woman was her own
children's grandmother. That had to stand for something. Suddenly she wasn't angry anymore, just cross
and sad. "You're bitter, Adele. I wish you weren't. I
know you don't like me, you never have. I can't change
the way you feel about me. But what about Pete and
Caroline and Sara? They're extensions of Clive, the
good parts of him. He still lives in them. Why don't you
share some of their happiness, their growing-up years.
Time goes so fast."

"Time goes slow! You're so thoughtless. But that's
because you have your children. I wish you were dead.
I wish all of you were dead! I wish I had my Clive back."

In the silence that slammed down, the terrible words
seemed to hang in the air—ugly, spiteful, out of reach.
Rachel's throat constricted. She bit back the rage. Yet
some slipped out, making it difficult for her to shape
hoarse words. "Don't you ever say a thing like that to
me! Don't you ever! How evil you are, Adele, to wish
such a thing on innocent children. I suffered when Clive
died. I'm still suffering. And so are his children. Do you
think it's easy for them, being different from other children, having no father, being poor?" Her hands fluttered and shook. She shoved them deep into the pockets
of her skirt. "I wish things could be different between
us. I wish you liked me. I wish you'd let me like you. I
don't want to come between you and the children, but
I think you'd better go. Maybe—"

"You haven't heard the last of me, Rachel Wallis,"
Adele spouted, her face a stiff mask. "You think you're
going to teach in Hickory Grove? You won't. I'll see to

it. Gossip about you and that man is as thick as molasses. Folk won't want your kind teaching their kids."

Rachel's chin went up. She tried to concentrate on all the times that Adele had been pleasant to her. It didn't work, for they had never shared a warm relationship. Rachel had overlooked incidents and harsh words—first, for Clive's sake and later, for the children's. No more. She gave in to her fury. "That's Cameron, Adele. Rachel Cameron. Do your worst if it makes you feel better. I'll survive, and so will my children. That's what we are, survivors."

Rachel didn't move until the sound of Adele's car had faded away. Then she stood quite still, letting the cool mountain breeze caress her face, listening to the gentle murmur of the creek below. After a moment, because she needed them, she called the children and gathered them to her, hugging each one very hard and burying her face in their hair. The rounded chubbiness of babyhood had gone out of Pete and Caroline but not Sara, and she hugged the baby's softness to her breasts. She wanted the children to stay just the way they were, not to grow up and drift away from her.

Pete rubbed his ear where she had planted a kiss. "Promise me you won't go doing anything so sissified in front of Billy, Mom. I wouldn't be able to hold my head up in school."

"You'll always be able to hold your head up," Rachel said fiercely.

"Gee, what's got into you?" he complained with immense masculine disgust.

"Personally, I like hugs," announced Caroline.

"You would!" her brother snorted, rolling his eyes.

"I love you all so much," declared Rachel, putting her arm around Caroline.

"You had another fuss with Grandma, didn't you?"

"I'm afraid so, honey. She was just in one of her moods."

"I think Grandma likes to fuss. I think she's happy when she's fussin'."

Rachel gave a short laugh. "You may be right, but don't say things like that. It's not nice."

"But I think it's the truth and you said—"

"Caroline Cameron, the truth is just something you need to know. You don't have to go around telling it. Now, as I recall, we have an agreement. Into the garden, all of you. There're squash and beans to pick, and about a million weeds that need pulling."

Once she had the children working, Rachel returned to the house and puttered around in the kitchen. The effects of her clash with Adele lingered. The summer heat seemed more oppressive, the humidity more stifling, the sweat that trickled between her breasts more acrid. She tried to bring forth a picture of Clive, but there was only a blank spot in her mind, a black hole that was filled with bitterness.

Were people talking about her, Rachel wondered. Hickory Grove was a small town and gossip was as much entertainment to its inhabitants as a good book or the eight o'clock movie on television. It could get out of hand. She didn't like to admit it, but the wrong kind of gossip could indeed hurt her chances with the school board. She sat down at the table once again to compose the letter, and this time she did not let thoughts of Garrett Stark intrude.

10

"DID YOU LET MAMA TALK on the radio when she went in your car?" Pete asked Garrett. The boy was sitting on the floor, his back resting against the wall, while Caroline kept her distance, perching on the railing at the far end of the porch. Her thin legs hugged the smooth wood for balance.

Sitting next to her mother in the swing, Sara was getting antsy. Rachel gave a kick with her foot to set the swing in motion. Garrett was straddling a chair that had been brought from the kitchen, his arms resting along its back. He puffed on his cigar and kept on staring at Rachel, probing for some sign from her—a sign that said she remembered their shared passion, that said she wanted more of him. His eyes met hers in a surge of frustration. "Is this a new game we're playing?"

Rachel looked down at her lap and chose another bean to snap. She knew he wanted to scatter the children so that he could talk to her, be alone with her. She raised her head, her smile fixed. "I don't know what you're talking about."

He did not smile back. A vein in one temple pulsed. His eyes, those light-colored eyes so darkly and thickly fringed, were lightless bits of stone. In the next instant he was addressing Pete.

"Would you like to show your sisters how a police radio works?"

The boy was up in a flash. "Can we talk into it for real?"

"As long as you don't push the button down."

"I don't want to play with any old radio," said Caroline.

"Suits me," said Pete. "A police radio is a man's job, anyway. Girls don't understand the mechanics."

It was a sideways challenge that got to Caroline. "I'm smarter than any old boy, especially you, Pete Cameron." With a toss of her head she slid from the railing, following her brother to the patrol car. Before Rachel could command her otherwise, Sara scooted from the swing, her chubby legs pumping to catch up with Caroline.

"Now, then," said Garrett, putting on a long face that exaggerated every expression. "You've been acting like a one-legged mule with a field to plow since I got here. You mad because I haven't been in touch?"

Rachel flashed him her remote-control smile—the one she used on the children when they thought being heathenish was cute. "No. What makes you think that? We don't have—are you feeling guilty about something?"

"That's just like a woman." He twirled his cigar between his thumb and forefinger. "Saying one thing and meaning another. I've been busy. End-of-month reports and taking a dozen depositions from farmers about those damned wild dogs killing calves. Had to do it because they have to make an official report before they can file on their insurance. I missed you. If you had a telephone, you'd know it."

Rachel let her gaze drift past him, politely distant. She wanted him so terribly, with a savage and helpless need. Why was she afraid to let him know how she felt about him? Because she was alone, and didn't want to

be? Because she knew now relationships didn't last?
People could drift apart or death could—did!—end it
for you. "I don't want to see you anymore. I have too
many other problems to deal with right now. Adding
you to the list just creates more risk."

"Risk? You just lay it right out, don't you?" He was
scrutinizing her, almost as though he had never seen her
before and there was an odd intensity in his gaze. "You
don't mean it, though. We've been to bed together. It
was good. We . . . fit."

"I know we went to bed together. Don't remind me."
Snap went a bean, and another. Camouflage to hide
what it was costing her to tell him goodbye.

"Don't remind you?" Blank disbelief crept into his
voice. "You're teasing me. You've known from the first
how to rile me. I can't think of any other reason for you
acting like this. Hell, I want to do it again. I've been
walking around with a ha—"

"Don't be vulgar."

He muttered an oath under his breath. The way she
was sitting there, eyes alight, leading with her chin,
breasts rising and falling—alluring, winsome and oh-
so-correct and prim—called to some savage instinct in
him. Rachel's behavior was all sham. All trouble! "I got
it. You want it in pretty words. How about this: everytime I close my eyes I see us together in bed. I feel what
we did, how we did it. My hands start to tremble, my
gut begins to ache. A certain part of me begins to swell,
painfully rigid. . . . Is that nice enough for you?"

Rachel was shaken and trying not to show it. Her
fingers gripped the enameled pan in her lap. "There's
no need for you to be sarcastic. We . . . just succumbed
to a lonely impulse, that's all. You're making a big deal
out of nothing."

A smoldering anger suddenly flared in his eyes, bright and alarming. "Nothing! You're making me mad, Rachel Cameron. I don't call stripping down and gettin' buck naked in front of a woman, for a woman— nothing!" Unthinking, he bit down on his cigar. Too hard. In two, it tumbled down his chest to the floor. "Now look what you make me do. Damn!" Without getting up from the chair, he ground out the cigar with his boot.

"Does that mean you usually make love with your socks on?" She looked down at the crushed cigar. "You're going to burn up Lackawanna County with your carelessness."

His eyes narrowed to slits. "Oh, now you're getting around to complaining about my smokes. I can't abide that in a woman." He pushed his hat back and sulked. After a moment Rachel caught his smile, twisted, mocking. "It won't work," he said softly. "You keep trying to get me off focus. I'm sitting right here until you tell me what's causing your wild hair." His smile grew. "Or maybe I won't sit here. Maybe I'll just grab you—"

"Not in front of the children!"

"They're going to have to see me touching you sometime. I'm told that's healthy. It's supposed to be a good way for parents to teach their children about sexuality."

But, thought Rachel. *But . . .*

Adele's words came crackling into her ears like the spillover of some bad dream. She paused for a heartbeat, taking a deep breath. "They're talking about us in Hickory Grove." It sounded lame. But it hadn't sounded lame when it came from Adele. Rachel kept that foremost in her mind.

Garrett bristled. "They? Who're they?"

"Everybody, I guess. The garden club. Clive's mother came out here earlier this week. She was radiating righteous indignation. She said your mother said—" Rachel was suddenly aware that his expression was going hard again, lips narrowing into a thin line, eyelids dropping, a muscle jerking in his jaw.

"My mother had nothing but praise for you. She was impressed with how neat and clean your house is, how mannerly the kids are. If she said anything, it was that. Adele Cameron twisted her words, but you ought to have known. Adele twists everything. She's one of Hickory Grove's own, so she's tolerated. Folk take what she says with a grain of salt. So should you."

"I didn't mean that your mother—"

"What did you mean?"

"Only that . . . Adele said she'd . . . she's going to complain to the school board about me being immoral so that they won't hire me. I need that job, Garrett. That's why I can't see you anymore. They might ignore most of what Adele says, but they'll think, 'Where there's smoke, there's fire,' and with your reputation with women . . ." Rachel swallowed on a dry throat.

"I see. I'm the risk you can't take. And what's my reputation with women?"

"Everyone says you've slept with every skirt between eighteen and forty in Lackawanna County."

"Do they? Well, I haven't—and more's the pity," he added with mock despair.

"Whatever they say, it's good for you and bad for me." She glanced out over the clearing, at the patrol car where the children were hunched in the front seat, at the thick underbrush where it met the soaring pines. She did not look at Garrett. "I think I'm in over my head. I don't want to pursue this conversation."

"Naturally not," he replied acidly. Garrett could always think on his feet and make split-second decisions under fire, but here he was in such a fog over Rachel, he could barely put two sentences together. Damned wrong sentences at that. Now Rachel, having set aside the beans, was holding her slim fingers entwined in her lap. He could very clearly, very precisely see those fingers trailing over his shoulder, his chest, his stomach.... A soft involuntary sigh escaped him.

"Will you please go now?"

With utter reluctance Garrett let go of the image in his mind. "No. I have another hour to spare and I mean to spend it here, with you."

Helplessly, Rachel glared at him. "I'll bet that no one ever bragged to your mother that you were mannerly."

"Now you're hurting my feelings. For that, you pay. And there's only one acceptable price." With swift grace he swung off the chair, grabbed her hand, pulled her out of the swing and propelled her into the house. Rachel had time for one pensive glance over her shoulder at her children, still playing in Garrett's car, and one surprised breathless, "Damn you!" She was starkly aware of being frantic for him and knew that once touched, once kissed, all her protesting would go for nothing.

"I don't like hearing you swear, Rachel. Some things are better left to men." He pinioned her arms and hauled her roughly against him. "Rachel, Rachel," he uttered throatily, "you do things to me without half trying . . ." His first kiss was tentative, his lips barely brushing hers. A tiny sip of nectar, no more—yet more than enough to cause hot blood to swell his sex in a throbbing arousal.

Snared in his bear hug, the feel of Garrett's hard male body against hers, Rachel was suddenly weak with raw desire. He nibbled at her lips, sucking gently as if fearful to let all his emotions loose in one fell swoop. "Tell me to stop now . . ."

"I want to." She moved her mouth over his face, feeling faintly the bristle of his whiskers against her sensitive lips.

"But you can't. I knew you couldn't hold out indefinitely against my method of torture."

"Police brutality of the worst kind," she murmured, drawing his head down so that her lips could brush his eyelids, his brow. A spiraling white-hot pleasure soared and sank, the hunger in her loins growing more insistent. "I don't want to be doing this. It's wrong . . ."

His hands traveled down her spine and lower, cupping firm flesh to press her urgently against the bulge between his thighs. "Lord, Lord," he breathed. "And to think we started out not liking each other."

Rachel stopped what she was doing, leaning back in his arms to create an inch or two of space so that she could look at him, his face, his eyes. "You really didn't like me at first?"

His laughter was low, teasing, and though he allowed her the distance between his chest and hers, he kept his hips pressed firmly, insinuatingly against hers. "I liked you as much as you liked me."

"But . . . I despised you!"

He kissed her on the tip of her nose. "It's a cross we'll just have to bear."

"You're laughing at me."

"I'm trying to make love to you. Standing up. With all my clothes on. That's laughing?"

"You know what I mean. What . . . what made you start liking me?"

His mind went at once to the image of her stalking up the path from the creek, her blouse wet and clinging to upthrusting breasts so that her pink nipples were delineated. Pink nipples that seemed to him were just begging to be fondled and sucked. But, good crying damn, he couldn't say that. She'd hold it against him for the next fifty years. "I don't know. You're feisty, for one thing. And you're good with your kids. That makes a man notice."

"I don't believe you." She wriggled against him, trying to get out of his arms.

He tightened his grip on her. "That feels wonderful."

"You're oversexed past belief," she told him.

"Now, hold on a minute," he said, stung by her comment. "How would you feel if I cuddled up to you like this and stayed as flat and limp as a tapeworm?"

She looked at him, saw he was serious and, letting her head fall helplessly against his chest, she laughed. "A tapeworm, Garrett?"

"Not romantic?"

"Wonderfully romantic," she said, and lifted her lips to his for exploring. His mouth crushed hers, his tongue finding the thrusting rhythm in that moist sweetness that another part of him ached for and went begging.

Rachel was about to faint from lack of oxygen when he finally dragged his lips from hers in a series of little biting nips. Wisps of hair had strayed from the ribbon that held it back and off her neck. Garrett wound a strand around his finger. The delicate rust-brown wisp looked incongruous against his rough calluses. "To-morrow is on, certain? You're taking the children to my mother's?"

"Yes. Around two o'clock."

"I'll be here about eight."

"I haven't heard myself inviting you."

"It's your turn to cook. Besides, I wouldn't think of letting you stay here all by your lonesome."

"What makes you think I would? You're taking a lot for granted."

"With you? That's a laugh. I never know if you're going to charge me with a broom or poison my food."

"Poison . . . ?"

"It crossed my mind once, back in the days when you didn't like me. Of course, I don't think that now, or I wouldn't be coming to dinner." A low moan escaped him. "I don't know how much longer we can keep standing here like this."

"Then turn me loose."

"Hate to," he said after a long time. But then he had to because they heard a giggle, and found Sara staring at them, her nose pressed flat against the screened door.

"Ah, well, I have to go anyway."

Rachel ushered Sara to the sink and washed the child's face and hands. "Wait for me on the porch," she said to Garrett. Then she put Sara at the table with crayons and a coloring book.

"Am I getting another kiss, to hold me over until tomorrow night?" he asked when she joined him.

"No. I—Garrett, you're not using me, are you?" There was a sudden tightness in her tone. It was foolhardy to ask such a question, and yet . . . On her part, she thought that they were involved in more than a light forgettable affair. It was getting so complicated.

"What provoked that?" He sounded angry.

"I have to know."

He shook his head. "I don't think I'm using you. But sometimes I feel like we're in the middle of a war. I'm taken with you," he embellished guardedly. "I'd admit that to anybody." He picked up his hat from the chair, slapping it against his thigh. He cleared his throat. "Just so you'll know. I'm not about to leap everytime you say frog."

She stiffened. "I feel the same way."

He wasn't so sure of her now. "Till tomorrow?"

Her smile did not reach her eyes. "Till tomorrow."

He went down the steps. "Eightish?"

"Fine."

He put on his hat, adjusting the brim low over his eyes. He was seeing the trap and walking right into it. "I'm pretty sure I'm not using you." He had a thought. "Ought I ask that of you?"

Rachel's sexual needs were ascending, not waning. She caught her breath, bit her lip and shrugged. "I've been lonely—very lonely—often."

"Which means you don't know whether or not you—" He clamped his jaws together. For hell's sake! He was about to say *whether or not you love me.* "Never mind," he grumbled, as if the thought didn't matter a whit. He stood in the relentless sun, looking at her for a long instant through glazed bemused eyes, then he spun on his heel and strode to the cruiser.

Suffering a mixture of misery and excitement, an emotional pressure so intense that she felt her head aching at the nape of her neck, Rachel watched his departure. He chatted with Pete and she could read her son's body language. It said Pete was thrilled with the sheriff's attention. Not so Caroline, who stood by her brother eyeing Garrett with youthful disdain. By no stretch of the imagination could it be said that her daughter was pleased with the sheriff's attentions to her mother. Thank heavens, thought Rachel, that it had not been Caroline who discovered her and Garrett in each other's arms. That was a problem she was not yet ready to handle, emotionally or practically.

SATURDAY DAWNED clear and hot. In her note to Martha Stark Rachel had promised to have the children at the Stark home by two o'clock so that Pete would have plenty of daylight to mow the lawn. There were dozens of tasks to be accomplished before she could bundle the children into the car, several of which brought strident protests from her brood. Only Caroline would sit still to have her bangs trimmed. Sara squiggled, and Pete yelled, and now he was on the sofa, sitting on his hands.

"I don't want you to file my nails, Mom. It's sissy. Besides, it sounds worse than chalk squeaking."

"I'm getting put out with you, son. Your nails are ragged and dirty."

"I'll clean them with my pocketknife, but they're just going to get dirty again. I'm working today, y'know."

Rachel threw up her hands. "Do it, then. And they had better be clean!"

Sunday clothes had to be ironed. Buttons replaced, a loose sash mended and each outfit put on a hanger with socks and underwear pinned together. Rachel ironed their pajamas, something she had never done before. The only suitcase she owned was in the shed out back and it was much too big. Paper sacks had to be employed for packing and names crayoned on.

"We know what belongs to who," said Caroline.

"Mrs. Stark doesn't."

At the last minute when she was herding them out the door, she had to stop and write out the party invitations for the next Saturday. In the wake of Garrett's leave-taking yesterday, she had forgotten. The children gave up a collective groan. "Never again!" complained Rachel, rubbing her temples.

They were at the end of the switchback road and turning onto the highway when Sara began to whimper. "She forgot Miss Mossy," said Pete.

Biting her lip to keep from screaming, Rachel backed up and knocked over her mailbox post. "Oh, great!"

The Starks lived on the old river road behind the tourist camp. Rachel felt blessed when she pulled into the driveway in front of the neat whitewashed house. She eyed the garage, the room above it, but there was no sign of Garrett. *Just as well,* she thought. She was frazzled and in no mood for flirting or the emotional upheaval he caused in her.

Martha Stark came out of her house wearing a big smile and a ruffled pink apron over her cotton dress. "You made it," she beamed, her smile taking them all in.

"I didn't think we would for a while there," Rachel confided with a rueful laugh. But then Mrs. Stark made a fuss over the children, commenting on how neat, how shiny they looked and Rachel felt all the trouble had been worth it.

"I have ice-cold soft drinks and peanut butter sandwiches all ready," she announced. "After that, why we'll get busy. Rachel, you'll stay for a soft drink, won't you?"

"That sounds good." She found herself reluctant now to go off and leave her babies behind. Yet, after ten minutes of polite conversation and light pleasantries in Mrs. Stark's fan-cooled kitchen, she heard herself saying goodbye, have a good time and behave yourselves. And, of all things, she had the oddest feeling that the children were anxious to see her go, as if Mrs. Stark was their newfound friend and not to be shared.

11

RACHEL REMOVED HER SHOES and sprawled across her bed. The summer breeze, drenched with pine and sliding in beneath the mulberry tree, soothed her body. It was strange being on the homestead alone. A luxury to be able to lie down in midafternoon for a nap with only the clucking of chickens for company.

Thinking of the coming evening with Garrett left her at sixes and sevens so that she dozed fitfully, feeling not at all refreshed when she awoke. However, lingering images of their moments alone yesterday energized her as the nap had not.

She put the small house to rights, planned dinner, set the table for two and found herself humming as she peeled eggplant and braised ground beef for Almost Moussaka. Not fancy perhaps, but filling, though she herself had no appetite.

She soaked in the tub until her skin wrinkled, then massaged it with lotion until it plumped up again. She shampooed her hair and let it dry in the sun while she sat on the porch manicuring her nails, all twenty of them. Thinking she was probably becoming a loose woman, she put on a freshly ironed gauzy blouse and shorts, disdaining underwear. On second thought, she mused, biting her full lower lip, she did have an appetite, an out-and-out craving. But not for anything that could be plucked from her garden, or satisfied by an overactive imagination.

If Garrett missed her like he said he did, wanted her the way his hard body promised, he would be early. She just knew it. By seven o'clock she was sitting in the swing on the porch in a rosy glow of anticipation while the sun grew frail, the mountain cooled and shadows lengthened.

Eight o'clock came . . . and went.

So did eight-thirty. Between then and nine o'clock, Rachel's ire rose with the sliver of moon. When Garrett finally sped into the yard and braked to a stop in a cloud of dust, she was too angry to be relieved.

"Is this what you call 'eightish'?" She lashed out at him, her arms folded across her chest hiding the delectables she had meant to flaunt.

"Be reasonable, Rachel. It's tough for me to get a Saturday night off. I didn't want to be late. There was a ruckus at Nester's and afterward I had to go home and clean up. You wouldn't want me coming out here smelling sharper than a skunk, would you? Then I spent a few minutes with the kids. They're having a good time. Pete got the lawn mowed . . ."

"But dinner . . ." Rachel said, softening.

He stood at the bottom of the steps, looking up at her in the moonlight, grinning. "Dinner be damned. It's you I want."

She moved her hands to her hips. She had softened, but she hadn't melted entirely. "You invited yourself to dinner and you'll eat it!"

His eyes locked onto the rosettes thrusting against the thin material of her blouse. "Punishment?" he said dourly.

"I've always been told the way to a man's heart is through his stomach," she said sweetly, turning her back on him and entering the house.

"The way to my heart is a few inches lower."

Her heart gave just the tiniest lurch. "Now, Garrett, don't sulk. I get enough of that with the children."

He hung his hat on the back of a chair and took a place at the table. "It smells good anyway. I don't suppose you have cold beer."

"Kool-aid." She gave him a wonderful smile and poured him a tall glass.

"Oh boy," he said glumly. "Cherry. My favorite."

She served up dinner, a huge helping of the eggplant entrée for Garrett, a meager one for herself, a great bowl of sliced zucchini-and-radish salad for him, a dab for her. He stared at her plate, then his own. "You're not playing fair, Rachel."

"Tit for tat, I always say. Dig in."

"I'm getting just a little bit mad."

"Don't," she said warningly, eyes alight.

"Into the spirit of things." He exhaled heavily and began to eat.

Rachel made no attempt at conversation while Garrett ate. She was almost sorry for her behavior—almost, but not quite. Not when he was pretending indifference yet tracking her every move, his eyes often alighting on her breasts. Her throat began to close and when she couldn't swallow another morsel, she moved from the table. "I made a mayonnaise cake. I thought we could have coffee and cake on the porch. Mosquitoes aren't too bad tonight."

He put down his fork, pushing his plate a small distance across the table. Then he looked up at her, a vein throbbing dangerously in his temple. "Game's over, Rachel. The coffee sounds good. I don't want any cake."

He left the room, carrying a chair onto the porch. When Rachel took his coffee to him he was leaning back in the chair against the wall, smoking an after-dinner cigar. Silently, he took one of the cups from her. She sat in the swing, suddenly bereft of words, thinking he was right. The game was over. She tilted her head back, closing her eyes for a moment to hurry night vision.

For a long while neither spoke. They shared the silence—waiting—as if silence was solid, a thing, a laggard being urged to a faster pace.

"It's beautiful up here." Garrett spoke finally, sounding as though his voice was backing up. "It was nights like this that I remembered when I was away. Just a rocker of a moon, yet the stars so bright you could find your way even in shadow, a creek running, sounding like silver in your pocket . . . whippoorwills calling." He sighed. "I never heard a whippoorwill in all the years I was gone."

"You talk as if you were homesick a lot."

"No, not a lot. Marines keep you too busy for that. But now and again . . ." His cigar had gone out. He flipped it into the yard. His need for her struck him like a tangible physical blow, and the force of want drove the breath back into his throat. "Rachel . . ." he said, oddly gentle.

"What?"

"Take off your clothes."

She started, taking a moment to absorb his command, still not believing what she'd heard. In the starlight she could see his mouth was thin lipped and tense, the muscles working under the skin of his square jaw. His eyes were hollow, but open and devouring her. "What did you say?"

"Take off your clothes."

"You—you're joking."

"No."

"Garrett . . ."

"I want to see you naked in the moonlight. I want to touch you, I want you to stand before me, let me touch you, let me take you onto my lap...." His voice was growing deeper, husky. "I want you right here, right now... I want to be inside you. I want to kiss your eyes, your throat, I want to feel your breasts on my tongue, suck your nipples—"

He was making love to her with words. Only words. Rachel felt a spreading warmth in her groin, felt it creep like gossamer threads of fire until it encompassed her entire being. Refusal lodged in her throat where it had no hope of forming verbal protest. "You're crazy," she whispered, even as her fingers trembled at the buttons of her blouse.

He was watching her, tracking the progress of her fingers as she shed her shirt, her shorts. But not listening, for he was disrobing, too. Boots, socks, belt, shirt, slacks until there was a rumpled pile at his side where he continued to sit. All four legs of the chair were now firmly on the rough porch floor. "Come over here," he said.

Rachel hesitated to move from the swing, certain that she would faint. Moon and starlight bathed his face, his corded neck, the broad shoulders, the ridge of muscles down his chest, the towering inflexible staff of his manhood.... Rachel drew in her breath and held it. She must have gotten out of the swing, taken a step toward him, because he said, "Turn around," and she did while he gazed, as a man might view a mirage he thinks, hopes, is real.

A muffled sound erupted from his throat. He reached for her hands, placing them on his shoulders.

"Garrett..." His name was an uncertain plea—to stop, to explain, to hurry. She felt his knees graze the sides of her legs. She had wine in her veins, she could soar on drunken wings.

"Shhh . . . don't talk. I'm making a dream real." His voice was low and hoarse. She could smell his hair, faintly imbued with the scent of his soap and his old hat. Beneath her hands, his shoulders were taut as wire, hard.

Rachel shut her eyes tightly. It seemed an eternity before she felt his hands on her, his fingers lightly touching her arms, trailing upward, across her shoulders, the hollows of her neck, and down. His strong fingers brushed her nipples—maybe she imagined it— in a feather-light touch, but then the pressure grew and she gasped.

"Perfect, perfect..." were words swirling around her. And Rachel thought, *he's not talking about me.*

His hands moved like rough silk over her hips, down the sides of her legs, rounding to the back of her knees, stopping a heartbeat before beginning their upward journey, curving slowly, ever so slowly until . . . his thumbs reached the soft inner folds of her femininity.

Her legs were not going to hold steady much longer. They couldn't. Her bones were melting, soft marrow centers pooling at her feet. The stars were closing in on her, crushing her. She held incredibly still waiting for his thumbs to move, waiting to begin that soaring, that rise to ecstasy. She almost spoke, stopping because his head came forward, his tongue flicked out, circling a swollen nipple. His first suck was gentle, the second caused a thrilling pulsating sensation to charge through her. She could no longer support herself and as her legs gave away, Garrett's hands moved, clutching her hips, pulling her forward, guiding her. She felt the engorged length of him begin to penetrate her. Her muscles contracted involuntarily and he moaned, "No, Rachel, no . . . wait."

She begged him to hasten the thrust, but his hands, his arms grew taut with strength, slowing the downward progress of her body. She bent to kiss his brow, his eyes, her tongue flicking at his earlobe. She bit at the soft flesh she found there, sucking on it. An oddly strangled gasp erupted from him and his hands pushed her, helping her until he was fully sheathed in her moist hot flesh.

For a minute, an hour, an eternity, neither moved. "Am I too heavy for you?" asked Rachel, her tongue thick.

"If I said yes?"

"You'll just have to suffer," she told him and those were the last words she could speak, for his arms encircled her, and she could feel their strength, feel bulging steely muscles bruising her back while her thighs moved rhythmically upon the solidity of his flesh. Never before had Rachel imagined such utter separation of her will from the independent will of her body. Right or wrong, the sensations engaging her senses now demanded surfeit. Droplets of perspiration beaded her forehead, her shoulders, her breasts, a lubricant for his hands, his tongue, his mouth as his passion mounted.

He was defenseless against the onslaught of all that she was, defenseless to resist the great physical attraction that was like an addiction. Ardor overtook him, turning back upon itself until he was vaulting to the pinnacle. "Rachel..." Her name was a plea, succor, an eruption of deep pleasure, and Rachel heard herself making some little animal sound as she sucked in deeply....

HIS ARMS STILL encircled her. She lay with her head on his shoulder for a time. Finally she raised her head. "I didn't think that...I mean it *never* is the second time..."

The disbelief was there and she was trying to shake it. "On the porch, too. Suppose someone had . . . ? I don't understand how I let you talk me into acting so crazy."

"You like me?" he said, feeling her out.

"Everytime I see you, I tell myself I won't again."

"When do you do this telling? Before or after?"

"I just remembered why I don't like you!" She pulled away, but not too far, for his hands captured her. "Turn me loose. I want to bathe and get my clothes on."

"I forbid you to put on a scrap."

"You forbid? You forbid!"

"Bathing is fine. Let's wash off our sweat in the creek."

"No way. Naked? Anyway, I don't have the strength to walk that far. Let's get back to 'forbid.'"

"I do," he said, grasping her thighs and moving her off him so that he could gain his feet. Then he scooped her up into his arms. His legs were a little wobbly. "On second thought, you weigh more than I figured." He let her legs trail until her feet touched the floor. "Guess you'll have to walk after all. But you can lean on me."

Rachel was torn between protesting that she didn't weigh much at all and being shepherded nude across the clearing and down the path.

"A swim will revive me," Garrett was saying.

"You can't swim in White Hawk Creek. It's not more than two feet deep. You can't forbid me to do anything."

"I wouldn't dream of it. Splashing around will revive me."

"This conversation is going at cross-purposes. And you don't look like you need reviving!" In the moonlight she could see that his sex remained rigid, hugging his abdomen.

He halted several yards from the rippling water and stepped in front of her. His hands touched her shoulders, moving down her arms, up again to caress her breasts. "I've been trying not to look at you, to keep my hands off you, but if you insist on pointing out the obvious . . . I'll lay you down and take you right here."

"You wouldn't!"

"Look again and tell me that."

Rachel kept her chin up. "Let's . . . let's go paddle around."

Garrett laughed. "I thought you'd see it my way."

Hours later as she lay with her head on his shoulder, sheets tangled about her feet, Rachel wondered drowsily if she'd dreamed up the entire evening. After they had rinsed and cavorted in the cool creek, Garrett had taken her again. She could, even now, lying in her own bed, recall the feel of the earth on her bare back. Her hand trailed up his thigh, over his stomach, and she ran her fingers through the wiry hair of his chest. She wasn't dreaming now. "Garrett, are you awake?"

"No."

"You can't stay here all night."

"I can't?" He groaned sleepily and shifted on the bed, tugging her closer. "Get me up and get me dressed and I'll leave."

Against her better judgment she snuggled deeper into his arms, lamenting softly, "You're the most impossible man I know."

"The only man," he replied with a proprietary air, and that was all he was going to say until he could sort out his feelings. He was considering that he was in love. Real love. It had never happened before. He wondered how he could be sure. It was a thing that had to be examined in the light of day. For the moment, his belly was full, the bed was warm and he was pleasantly sated. He planned to put off leaving as long as possible. Yawning widely, he buried his face in Rachel's hair.

"Now I know the secret of your wonderful charm," she muttered. "You haven't any." With that she turned over, giving him her back. Smugly pleased, Garrett rolled in her wake, curling tightly against her back and buttocks.

RACHEL STARED at her reflection in the bathroom mirror, seeing in a peripheral way that her cosmetics were not overdone, that her chestnut hair was smoothed back and held in place by a barrette at the nape of her neck. Her eyes were not so much on her own reflection as they were gazing inward into a realm beyond reason. She was in love with Garrett Stark. It went beyond sex, although sex with him was better, far more satisfying, than it had ever been with Clive. That's how she knew she loved him. She could think things like that now without feeling guilty about them.

Being in love did not solve her problems. There was still the shortage of money, the need to find work and the children to consider. Combined, they compared to the heavy sword suspended by a hair over Damocles. Still, for the moment she was happy. Exultant! In love! In a mood where nothing mattered except to laugh; where relations and work and debts suddenly became as light as feathers and as buoyant.

Tomorrow could take care of itself.

Then Garrett was banging on the bathroom door. "Coffee's ready, or do you plan to be in there past dinner?"

Emerging from the bathroom, Rachel's smile was serene. "It's a beautiful Sunday morning, and you're a grouch."

"You were squandering our last few minutes together."

"Shall we have our coffee on the porch?"

"In the house. I want to watch you dress."

Rachel tightened the sash of her robe. "No, I know where that will lead. I don't want to be late picking up the children." She tried not to show it, but Rachel reveled in the fact that a touch from her, or an accidental glimpse of cleavage could make his manhood, however quiescent it lay, begin to swell and clamor for attention.

But Garrett was not to be talked or teased out of this pleasure he had set for himself.

"It's one thing for you to watch, another for you to inspect!" wailed Rachel as Garrett sat on the bed not two inches from her as she attempted to pull on stockings.

Garrett's hand shot out, staying her. "Take off the robe first."

The sun was streaming in the window. Rachel hesitated. Up to now Garrett had made no mention of her stretch mark. In the daylight it was there on her hip, too easily discerned, ugly and puckered. She reached for her coffee on the bedside table and took a sip, stalling. "Suppose I don't want you to see me?"

"Then you'd better suppose something else."

If the stretch mark turns him off, Rachel thought, *it's better to know now.* And even if it did, he couldn't take back what had already gone between them. With a pensive shrug she loosened the belt and let the robe fall from her shoulders.

Garrett held his breath. Rachel's beauty coupled with her momentary shyness made him want nothing more than to hold her. He touched the puckered skin on her hip, letting his finger trail lightly down its length. "Is this why you've been turning away from me in the least bit of light?"

She nodded.

"It's a badge of motherhood, isn't it?"

"You've seen stretch marks before?" The taint of jealousy was in every word.

He took a shallow breath. Inmates in the county jail had a saying: never tell the truth when a good lie will suit. "Being a cop, you see everything," he said easily.

"Of course."

"I don't mind at all about the stretch mark, if that's what's been worrying you."

"Well, that's a good thing, isn't it? Because I can't undo it." She sat down again and this time, did get her stockings on, then her underwear, the pink blouse she had chosen and a belted white skirt. "Seen enough?" she asked, managing to infuse a wealth of sarcasm in the two-word query.

Garrett glared at her for several seconds, then moved off the bed, striding across the room to slam and latch the side door. He headed for the front.

Rachel's hand fluttered uselessly toward him. "What—what are you doing?"

"What does it look like I'm doing?"

"I can see . . . that's not what I meant."

"You mean my intentions? Well, hell, my intention is to lock these doors, then rip every scrap of cloth off your body and assault you. That's my intention."

"You're angry."

"Got it right on the first try."

"But why?"

"Because every time I get ready to leave you, you start a fight. Not today. You don't like the idea of me having known other women. That's unreasonable. For hell's sake. I'm thirty-eight years old! What am I supposed to have been doing all these years? Just holding limp until I found—" Hearing what he was saying, he stopped in midsentence.

Rachel brushed past him, kicking open the front screened door. "Out! You're beyond conceit, Garrett Stark. I don't care if you've had a woman once a day and twice on Sunday since you were in diapers!"

"I see through that."

"You don't see past your nose! I just don't want you talking, bragging about your prowess with me."

Garrett gaped. "You think I—?" His light-colored eyes went glacial. Rachel reached for his hat and tossed it to him.

"Goodbye, Sheriff Stark."

He examined her face carefully. "Well, you did it. I'm going off mad."

"I'm crushed."

"You're screwy in the head." He slammed the smelly old felt hat on his head, and snapped the brim—which had very little snap left—at a swaggering angle. The gesture was by now very familiar to Rachel. And maybe a little dear. She softened, giving him a bright steady stare, her mouth whimsically awry.

"I'm sorry we didn't have time for breakfast."

He ran his hands over his jaw, down his cheek. "Or a shave." There was a quick roguish flash of his eyes, an ironic grin, but a grin nevertheless. "Fight's over?"

"Seems like it. Would you like to kiss me goodbye?" Then she was beside him, tempting . . .

Their mouths joined, their bodies pressing together. His hands glided over her back and down to her hips.

Rachel felt him growing hard against her and reached down to touch him.

He moaned, whispering a warning, "Keep that up and you'll never make it to Mother's."

Rachel removed her hand, wondering how she was ever going to live without him now.

On her way to reclaim her small brood, Rachel suffered a twinge of anxiety. Had they missed her? Were they all right? Had Sara been happy or forlorn? And Martha Stark—was she at this very minute regretting having asked the children to visit?

The questions in her mind made Rachel drive faster than was her wont. The old station wagon protested the speed with rattles, thunks and knocks, and a trail of burning oil smoke erupted from the tail pipe. When she pulled into the Stark driveway, Pete, Caroline and Sara waved gaily from their perch on the porch steps. Each was neatly groomed and dressed for church. Rachel let loose a relieved sigh.

She hugged Caroline and Sara, but Pete skittered out of reach. Rachel glanced over their heads to Mrs. Stark. "Any problems?"

"Not a one. Can you take time for coffee? We can sit in the chairs in the yard, now that Pete has the lawn mowed so nicely."

"I will. Thanks." She turned to Pete. "Why don't you gather up yours and your sisters' things and put them in the car."

"We got a lotta loot, Mom," he shrilled. "We cleaned out the attic. I got a whole set of marbles, a slingshot and a train engine that really works!"

"All junk!" claimed Mrs. Stark, returning with the coffee. Rachel laughed, accepting the proffered cup.

"But a treasure trove to the children. If I asked them to clean out a drawer at home, they'd pitch a fit."

"You know how it is, strange closets and attics hold all sorts of mystery."

"I got a diary, Mama. It only has two used pages."

"That's wonderful, Caro."

"And I talked on the phone to Janice Sizemore. Mrs. Stark let me."

"Are you sure they weren't any trouble?" Rachel asked the older woman again.

"They weren't. They were a lot of help. It was nice to have young bodies available to get into corners and closets. My old bones don't bend like they used to." She took a sip of coffee, looked away from Rachel and back again. "Garrett called from the office. He said you two spent the evening together."

Rachel's cheeks flared pink. "Yes . . . I . . . we did."

"I'm not trying to pry. I just wanted to mention that gossip sometimes has a person far more colorful than they really are."

"Meaning?"

Martha Stark shrugged her thin shoulders. "I would love for Garrett to settle down. I'd hate to see him lose out because of . . . He just acts so enthralled by you."

Rachel was thrilled with Mrs. Stark's assessment, but she was in an awkward position. To agree with Garrett's mother would be to appear immodest, not to agree was unthinkable. "He's been . . . nice to me, and the children," she added lamely.

"I'm sorry, I've gone off out-of-bounds, haven't I?"

Bemused and charmed by Mrs. Stark's contrite expression, Rachel smiled. "It's a mother's prerogative. We all want what's best for our children."

"Exactly!" Then Mrs. Stark reached out and touched Rachel's arm. "Also, I'd love to get Garrett out of my hair and into someone else's. He cramps my style. 'Do this, Mama. Don't go out after dark. Stay away from Nester's back room.' Heavens! I'm sixty-seven years old. Garrett behaves as if I'm two or worse—a hundred."

Laughing, Rachel set aside her cup and stood up. "I guess prerogatives work both ways. Thanks again for having the children. It was good for them. We're so isolated out on the homestead."

"Anytime, Rachel. I mean that. Of course, I don't want to step on Adele's toes. I imagine she wants her share of time with her grandchildren."

A quick glance in Mrs. Stark's direction told Rachel there was no malice in the other woman's comment. She stopped in midstride, casting about for something to say. "Actually, Adele doesn't take the children very often." Then, fearful that it might sound like criticism, she said, "She's a bit high-strung, especially since . . ."

"Of course, old fool that I am, I should have known. Well, I won't need any lunch what with all the shoe leather I've downed this morning, will I?"

"Now I know where Garrett gets his sense of humor," Rachel teased.

Mrs. Stark's remorse fell away. "That noxious wit he spouts is from his father."

All at once the children were surrounding them and hollering to go. "You didn't forget we've got to hand out the invitations before Sunday school?" Pete asked.

"No, I didn't. Say thank-you to Mrs. Stark for having you, then into the car and buckle up," she commanded.

After church, Evelyn Sizemore waylaid Rachel in the parking lot. "I just wanted to say yes! Yes! Yes! Janice can come to the picnic next Saturday."

"Summer's not getting you down, is it?" Rachel said with a laugh.

"Oh, no," Evelyn said wryly. "But if it was up to me, school would go on twelve months of the year." A pleasantly pretty woman, Evelyn Sizemore had a perpetual weight problem. She was forever dieting and buying clothes one size too small in anticipation of shedding pounds. She adjusted her print dress where it curled around her waist. She aimed her gaze at Rachel's shoulder. "Listen, we're all glad that you've come out of your shell, back to church and all . . ."

And all? Rachel wondered. "Thank you. It gets easier. I didn't think it would."

"That old adage about time, I suppose. You're dating now, I hear?"

Rachel stiffened. "No." Evelyn Sizemore's father was on the school board and the last person Rachel wanted to know of her liaison with Garrett Stark.

"Oh," said Evelyn. "I thought . . . I heard you and—"

"No," Rachel said, more firmly.

"Just gossip again," sighed the young mother. Yet the lift of an eyebrow suggested conspiracy. She was aching to be Rachel's confidante.

Determined not to let the sheriff's name pass her lips, adding fuel to fire, Rachel said nothing.

Quick to take the hint, Evelyn changed the subject. "Oh, I spoke to Gertie Evans. She said Billy and Lily had been invited. We decided between us that one of us would drive the kids out and the other pick them up. Is that okay with you? About ten in the morning? Right?"

"Noon to about seven, Evelyn." Rachel said, laughing, recovering her happy spirits. "Not a minute before or later. Or I'll be prostrate. You know the turnoff? The name's on the mailbox."

"I'll find it. I wish you'd thought of this before. At least, I'll have something to hold over Janice all week. By Saturday her room will be spotless!"

12

RACHEL SPENT the remainder of the afternoon at loose ends. She and Pete had repaired the downed mailbox, and that had been the last bit of help she had wrested from the children. Each was now enthralled with the loot they had brought home from Martha Stark's. Sara, sitting on the loft steps, was occupied dressing and undressing Miss Mossy in the new outfit Mrs. Stark had fashioned for the doll; dozens of times—at least it seemed so—Rachel was called upon to do and undo the buttons. Pete was scouring the banks of the creek for stones—ammunition for the slingshot. Caroline sat on the shaded front stoop, laboriously engaged in "keeping her diary."

Though she longed for a nap, Rachel couldn't bring herself to lie down on the bed. It seemed sinful that her every waking moment was filled with thoughts of Garrett. Wishing to lie abed in the middle of the afternoon just so she could dream about him made her furious with herself. Still, all afternoon she had worn a smile, as if some great secret was just out of sight. The children had plagued her with, "What's so funny, Mama?" until she had shooed them out to play on their own. All the same, she went about the house doing the things that mothers do, filled with a strange exhilaration.

"How do you spell 'horridest'?" asked Caroline when Rachel found herself standing at the screened door, gazing at everything and nothing.

"There's no such word. You must mean horrid."

"It isn't a word, it's a person," insisted Caroline.

"Which person?"

"Diaries are secret, Mama. I can't tell you."

"Is it somebody we both know?"

"It's somebody who's horridest," answered the child crossly.

Rachel went out onto the porch and sat in the swing. "Did this person hurt your feelings or something?"

Caroline closed the book, eyeing her mother with distrust. "You're not going to peek when I'm asleep, are you?"

"Of course not. If you want to have a secret from me, that's all right."

"But you're going to be mad about it?"

Rachel laughed. "No, I won't be mad."

"Good," said Caroline, opening the book and licking the end of her pencil. "How do you spell—"

"Now, wait a minute. You go look it up in the dictionary, like I showed you."

Caroline wrinkled her pert nose, the big eyes regarding her mother with feline softness under the brown mop of hair. "I hope you don't act like this when you teach or I won't have a friend in the world!"

"And I hope you don't sass your teachers or I'll be embarrassed."

The child slumped over her book for a minute, her little square mouth drawing down at the corners, a flush on her high cheekbones, her eyes throwing wary sparks. "Are you going to get married and leave us?"

"Caroline! No! I'd never leave you or Pete or Sara. Darling, I love you, all of you. I couldn't live without you."

"Could you live without Sheriff Stark?"

Rachel blinked as if she'd been slapped. Her mouth went horribly dry. She had never thought that she would be in the position of defending her emotions to her children. She felt a little sad and a lot upset. "I can live without Sheriff Stark, yes."

"Will you?"

Careful, Rachel told herself. She didn't want to say something now that she might regret later. "I think this conversation has gone far enough, Caroline. Whether I will or I won't is moot."

"I don't know 'moot.'"

"It means it doesn't matter, it means there are no choices to make—" She checked herself. Something in her daughter's pointed face and catlike eyes excluded her. *It means he hasn't asked me—us—to live with him. It means he hasn't said he loves me or that he doesn't. It means* . . . She closed her eyes, slumping back in the swing, suffering an escalating dreamlike sense of chaos.

When she opened her eyes, Caroline was gone. She considered calling the child back, but thought better of it. To continue the subject of Garrett Stark would put too much emphasis on him, on their relationship. But the wedge was there now, jammed between what was right and what she wanted. What she dearly wanted. She thought, if I'd just handled it right . . . if I'd said . . .

The exact words escaped her, but she could feel the conversation—light, airy, Caroline laughing as though they shared a secret about men. But that was too much, wasn't it, to ask of a seven-year-old who was feeling insecure?

Standing up, inhaling the odors of summer—heat and pine sap and chicken droppings—Rachel decided that if widowhood had a smell, that was it. Heavy-hearted, she went into the house to prepare dinner.

Ten minutes later, washing vegetables at the sink, it came to her. She knew who "horridest" was. She laughed softly. Well, she had called him worse, hadn't she?

"SIT DOWN!" roared Garrett to the giant of a man who was a shade over six-foot-three and whose frame exceeded two hundred and fifty pounds.

The rancher swayed drunkenly. "Haw! You gonna make me, Sheriff? You willow-stick heathen, you gonna make me?"

Reaching under his desk, Garrett brought forth a well-worn baseball bat. It had belonged to his father and was autographed by Babe Ruth. He would never use it on a man, but the old crock standing before him didn't know that. He laid it across his desk, gently, precisely, then tapped it before lifting his eyes to glare chillingly at the rancher, saying with utter calm, "Won't you have a seat, Mr. McKenzie?" Then he stuck a cigar in his mouth and rummaged around the top of his desk for a match as if the bat were invisible flotsam.

The man's eyes flicked from the bat to Garrett and back to the bat again. "That ain't playing fair, Sheriff." He sat and the chair gave away, splintering in a dozen pieces.

The dispatcher across the room snickered. Garrett scowled at the desk-bound deputy. The idiot! Laughing at the giant sprawled on the floor was just the thing that might make the situation unmanageable. Might also be just the incentive for the bulky rancher to mangle a sheriff beyond recognition. Inwardly, Garrett raged at the dispatcher's stupidity, but now McKenzie was stirring, demanding his full careful attention.

Dragging his great bulk to his hands and knees, the rancher's face metamorphosed from blank disbelief to rage. With a blunt finger Garrett inched the bat out over the desk until it touched the man's whiskey-reddened nose.

"Doesn't seem to be your day, does it, Mr. McKenzie." Shaking his head with mock solemnity, he signaled for the dispatcher to bring another chair. And damned quick.

"That was a cheap trick. You ain't goin' to be sheriff next election!"

"You're entitled to your vote, Mr. McKenzie, but for the time being, I'm the law. And I want you to tell me, in the nicest way you know how, just why you felt the urge to rough up the auctioneer at Buster's?"

"He sold my cattle short, that's why!"

"I saw your cattle, McKenzie. All together, they wouldn't make a good pot of soup. You want fat-cattle prices, you have to feed 'em."

"If you was doin' your job, them cows woulda been fat! I can't put 'em to pasture 'cause of the dogs running wild. They've et or crippled every single one of my summer calves. Every single one!" he boomed, venting whiskey-soured breath.

Garrett winced as the smell reached him. "We have an animal control unit working on the problem, but you farmers and ranchers have to do your share."

"Workin' on the problem?" McKenzie sneered. "How many of them dogs you shot or captured so far?"

"Two."

"Haw! Two out of a pack running a baker's dozen ain't workin', Sheriff. I'm payin' county taxes and I want my money's worth. It don't make no never mind to me whether I git it outen the auction house or your hide." His veined face puffed up. "Might be I'll get you sometime when you ain't got no bat, eh? Now, kin I go or what? My wife's waitin' for me over to Sears."

"You can go. But if Mr. Sapps files charges, you'll have to come in and post bond."

"He ain't hurt none."

"That's for him to decide. Meanwhile, Mr. McKenzie, I suggest you stop off at Nester's for coffee before you get on the road. You get behind the wheel of your rig liquored up and we'll just have to make you up a bed here."

"Like hell!"

Speaking softly, Garrett rubbed a blunt finger along the old tape wrapped on the bat neck. "That's what it'd be, friend—like hell."

McKenzie grunted a last-ditch reply, indecipherable, as he stalked from the station. Garrett watched his departure, noting the man's unsteady gait. To the dispatcher, he said, "Radio Slim. Tell him to take a coffee break at Nester's in ten minutes. If McKenzie isn't there, I want to know it."

"You wouldn't've used that bat on him, would you?"

"No, but I might use it on you if you ever crow like you did five minutes ago. Our job's to defuse a situation, not fuel it."

"Aw, I didn't mean nothin'."

"Famous last words," said Garrett pithily, returning the bat to the well of the desk beside the glove and hardball. All of which he planned to give to Pete Cameron. The boy had admired them when at his mother's, but Mrs. Stark hadn't been sure Garrett was willing to give them up. "Damnation!" he said suddenly. "I hate Tuesdays."

"What if they held auctions on Wednesdays?"

"Then I'd hate Wednesdays," Garrett spat.

"They'd never do that. Men 'ud be too drunk for church."

A crash came from the kitchen, another, then the old cook's voice rose tunelessly, shouting "The Old Rugged Cross."

"Oh, hell. Billy's got a load on." Wearing a grim expression and brushing both hands through his thick black hair, Garrett strode through the door separating the station from the jail proper. The smell of scorched food assailed his nostrils and half-cooked spaghetti was splattered on the floor in front of the stove. Billy Bass was on his knees, swirling the gummy mass with a rag.

"Sheriff!" the old man exclaimed, lisping the word so that it came out "theriff." His bald head was shiny with sweat. He looked at Garrett through an alcoholic haze. "'Twern't my fault, nosiree. That pot fair walked off the stove."

"Did it, now? Where'd you get the sugar, Billy?"

"I didn't steal it, nosiree, I didn't. You know old Billy Bass ain't no thief." The old man giggled through a hiccup.

Avoiding the mess as best he could, Garrett hauled the old drunkard to his feet and tried another tack. "You're a sly old hell-raiser, aren't you, Billy? Cooked up a pot of liquor right under my nose." He shepherded the old man to a bench, sat him down and pushed gently until the ancient spine was against a wall.

"Not liquor," boasted Billy. "Dandelion wine. With raisins."

"C'mon, Billy. There's no dandelions growing in this jail."

"Course not. But out to your lady's land was lots of 'em. Boys brought 'em back to me with that hog." He grinned crookedly. "Got 'em by the deputy 'cause they looked like weeds. Good weeds, though. Folk curse the dandelion for a weed, but not this child, nosiree." He leaned dangerously to the left.

"Nosiree," mimicked Garrett under his breath while throwing out a hand to keep Billy from falling. His lady. He hoped Rachel didn't get wind of that. Then he told himself he didn't care a whit about the gossip, but he knew it wasn't true. Where Rachel was concerned, he cared very much. Slim Walters had to be running off at the mouth. Damn him! Sailors always were a bad lot for scuttlebutt. He turned his attention to Billy again, coaxing. "You made wine with no sugar?"

"Had sugar." He was slurring badly now, his lids drooping, hiding the bloodshot eyes. "Was a present."

"A present?"

"From the wife."

Garrett groaned. Mrs. Bass was four foot high, rail thin and so sweet faced it gave lie to the streak of iron meanness that a torch couldn't cut. When she was tired of fooling with her husband or wanted to visit her grandkids in Kansas City, she put whiskey before him. After he was suitably inebriated, she'd turn him loose within smelling distance of a deputy. Then when her lawn needed tending or the plumbing went awry, she begged Billy out of jail on furlough. To his acute dismay, Garrett felt a creeping sadness for the old man. He half carried, half dragged Billy to his cot, then enlisted two other inmates to clean up the kitchen and prepare a meal.

The dispatcher looked up when Garrett slid behind his desk. "Slim says McKenzie showed up at Nester's with his wife. They had coffee and pie."

Garrett acknowledged the information with a nod. "Tell Slim to get on back here. He can hold the fort. I

have things to do." What he had to do was see Rachel.
Touch her, talk to her before he went out of his mind.

"COULDN'T YOU HUSTLE the kids to bed a few minutes
early?" He was leaning against the counter, watching
Rachel at the stove and keeping his voice low so it
wouldn't carry to the children at the table.

"No, they get a bedtime snack."

He smiled. "Do I get a bedtime snack, too?"

"Cinnamon toast and hot chocolate?"

"My appetite leans to something a bit more...fleshy."

"Cinnamon toast and hot chocolate or nothing," she
replied, taking down another cup.

"You're mean," he said, aware that Rachel was a little
too animated, a little too flushed. She carried the chocolate, frothy with melting marshmallows, to the table.
He followed her with the tray of toast.

"I suppose now that you have company, we have to
go straight to bed," said Caroline to her mother.

"You always go to bed after your snack. Tonight is no
different." Leaning down, she gave Caroline a light kiss
on top of her head. Where Pete had greeted Garrett with
high spirits, especially after being presented with the
bat, ball and glove, Caroline's greeting had been little
more than arched politeness, her pointed little face
bursting with resentment. Rachel sighed inwardly.
She'd have to explain to Garrett about showing par-
tiality with gifts or attention.

"Sometimes we sit on the porch afterward."

"I know we do, but not tonight." Rachel turned to
Garrett. "You want to sit at the table?"

"I think I'll wait for you on the porch."

"You goin' to be here when we get up, Sheriff?" asked
Pete with an unmistakable thread of hope.

"Why should he be?" injected Caroline. "He doesn't live here!"

Seeing a retort building in Garrett, Rachel held up her hand, an entreaty for him to remain calm.

"No, son, I'm not, I have an early—"

"He's not your son!" shrilled Caroline. "He's my daddy's son. You're just trying to take his place and you can't. Mama won't let you. She said so!" Caroline was trying hard not to cry.

Rachel's voice came muffled, jerky. "Go up to bed, Caroline, right now. You've said enough." She touched Garrett's arm. "I'll join you on the porch in ten minutes. I can explain—"

"That kid needs—"

"I know what she needs," hissed Rachel, tightening her grip on his arm, "and I said I'd explain. Now, please, wait for me on the porch."

He looked hard and long at her, then flung open the door and went out.

CLOUDS OBSCURED THE MOON, throwing the mountain into a purple darkness. Rachel wrapped her arms tightly around her middle and stood still, thinking. The chains on the swing creaked and groaned beneath Garrett's weight. She knew he was watching her, waiting. But the words she had planned to speak seemed suddenly pale and inadequate—none eloquent enough to explain what Caroline was suffering, what she herself was suffering.

"Hardly an hour has gone by that I haven't thought about you, Rachel."

"I've been thinking of you, too."

He moved behind her taking her in his arms and hugging her to his chest. "You're tense, or have you forgotten you're supposed to melt at my touch?"

Rachel rested her arms atop Garrett's, feeling their strength. "It's Caroline. She doesn't like you."

"Does she have to? As long as you do, I'm happy."

"But I saw you getting angry—"

"Because I sense that if you seeing me makes Caroline unhappy, or uncomfortable, you'd tell me to get lost."

"I wouldn't. We'd just have to be more careful in front of her, that's all."

"I wish you could hear yourself. You don't want to be seen in public with me, you don't want your children to have an inkling of our relationship.... What's left? Where do we go from here?"

"I don't know." Her heartbeat was chaotic. She wanted him to go. She wanted him to stay. His lips were very near her ear, his breath warm.

"I'm trying not to get mad, Rachel, but I won't be kept in the closet like an old pair of shoes."

"It's only until I get a teaching contract."

"Only until you get a teaching contract, only until Caroline comes around... Only! Only! Only!" He moistened his lips. "Suppose, just suppose, I was thinking about making ours a permanent relationship? How many 'onlys' would you put in the way of that?" The words were no sooner out of his mouth than he sensed a sudden inertia besiege her. He had the monumental insight that he had chosen the right question and the wrong time.

Rachel felt as if all of her limbs were suddenly weighted down with hundred-pound casts. She had to take several deep breaths before she turned in his arms, compelled to place her hands to his face. "It's too soon. Not for me. You've swept me off my feet, you know. But, for the children... Besides, you don't know what you'd be getting into." Doctor bills, dental bills, school clothes, PTA meetings, the bickering . . . Oh, there were lists on top of lists to scare a man away once he'd given it some thought.

Garrett's heart and pride were riven, his dignity wounded. He dropped his arms, freeing Rachel. He had never come that close to asking a woman to marry him. He wanted to assure her that being married to him would make her safe from gossip mongers. But he knew it wouldn't. There were no sacred cows in Lackawanna County. "Well, I was just supposing. But I can't help feeling that you're being damned selfish."

"Please," Rachel coerced, wondering how she could persuade him to take her into his arms again. "Be reasonable."

"I have no interest in being reasonable. Being reasonable means giving you up or sitting around twiddling my thumbs waiting for Hickory Grove to give up its number one entertainment. Being reasonable means sneaking around. Hell, I'm tired of being reasonable."

Heart twisting, Rachel yearned to say, "I love you." To beg for his strength, his hope, his love. "I think I could do with a smoke," she said.

He watched her light up, seeing the dismay etched in her face in the flare of the match. "Oh, hell! Put that thing out. You don't have anything against kissing, do you?"

"You know where that leads—"

He put an arm around her and his voice, when he spoke, was singularly dry. "Thank God some things never change."

When his hungry mouth claimed hers, Rachel, for a short time, consigned all her worries to a mental dustbin.

RACHEL BIT HER LOWER LIP, reading for the third time the reply from the school board. No permanent openings, but they would be delighted to have her sign up for substituting. Subbing! She'd be lucky to get three days' work a month. And here it was the first week in August, and no social security check, either.

She went to her small store of cash, kept hidden in a cigar box in the bottom of her dresser. Methodically, she counted and recounted. Two hundred and twenty dollars between herself and poverty. She wouldn't cry. She wouldn't let it get her down. As she smoothed the crumpled bills, a shivering seized her, seeming as if it could separate her flesh from her bones. She made up her mind. Next week, first thing Monday morning, she'd start at one end of town, at Hollister's Lumber Mill, and work her way to the tourist camp at the other. She'd find work, even if she had to wait on tables at Nester's! She'd ask Adele—no! never Adele—Mrs. Stark to watch the children.

She inhaled a defiant breath and let it out slowly. She felt better now, much better. And once she had a job, she'd tell Garrett they could parade arm in arm up and down Main Street. There had to be a way that Caroline could be wooed. If the child resisted... Rachel swallowed. The thought wasn't to be borne. She removed twenty dollars from the cache. For hot dogs, soft drinks and marshmallows. One summer picnic coming up!

THE SUN WAS AT ITS PEAK, creating shimmering heat auras that rose from the clearing to envelope the youngsters who were oblivious to it. Entrapped in the auras were the smells of dust and the dry mulch carpeting the forest floor.

"It must be twenty degrees cooler up here than it is in Hickory Grove," said Evelyn, plopping her rounded bottom down in the swing. "You have it made, Rachel. No wonder you're hardly ever in town. Groceries right out your back door, a swimming hole at the front. I love it!"

"Well, it's home," Rachel averred, swiveling on the porch railing to spy out the whereabouts of each of the children.

Sara and her companion for the day, five-year-old Lily Evans, were designing a playhouse in the dirt around the old tree stump. Pete and Lily's brother, Billy, were digging worms to bait cane fishing poles, while Caroline and her friend Janice were cutting out paper dolls at the table in the kitchen. Their girlish chatter, spiked with giggles, ebbed and flowed with the shaded breeze coursing through the house.

Evelyn nodded toward the stump. "Those two seem to have taken to each other quick."

"It's good for Sara to have a playmate her own age. I think I've been overprotective."

"You never did find out why she won't talk?"

"Had five different reasons from five different doctors. The last one said to keep her hollering and screaming so her vocal cords wouldn't atrophy and that she'd talk when she got ready."

Evelyn laughed. "So what's the therapy? Hair pulling and pinching?"

"Don't I wish!"

"You'll believe in corporal punishment by the end of this day, I'll warrant," warned Evelyn with a wry smile. "And I think I'll leave before you have second thoughts. I can't remember the last Saturday my husband and I had to ourselves. I might even be so grateful I'll borrow Caroline for an afternoon one day next week."

Rachel opened her mouth to say no, then changed her mind. If the girl had other interests to occupy her time, she might not spend so much of it being disagreeable about Garrett. "She'd love it. Would you like a soft drink or something before you head back home?"

"Nope, I'm dieting." She picked up the brown paper sack beside her on the swing. "You were too generous with your vegetables as it is. Fresh tomatoes, zucchini, eggplant, cukes, onions. I'm going to make this into a salad and pig out with no guilt."

"You've been on a diet since our senior year in high school, Evelyn. That's fourteen years. Have you ever actually lost any weight?"

Evelyn smiled, looking sly. "That's a nasty-nice question, Rachel. About as nasty-nice as me trying to find out if you're dating Garrett Stark."

"I retract the question."

"That's good, because I'd lie...just like you would."

There was more teasing than antagonism in Evelyn's tone. But Rachel was mortified and it showed. She had been determined to be friendly, casual, keep to ordinary subjects, never mind the difficulties. She had carelessly left herself open for Evelyn's remark. They had never been close friends, but not enemies, either. And now the woman's face was ripe with enthusiastic inquiry. It had to be deflected. She wasn't yet ready, Rachel told herself, to bare her soul.

"You don't have to keep looking at me as if I've lost all decorum," Evelyn was saying, looking aggrieved. "I was only giving tit for tat."

Rachel gave a small tart laugh. "Sorry. I got lost there a minute. Comes from being alone so much." She observed the boys for a moment, gathering her wits and the courage to ask a question and somehow retain her dignity. Oh, the hell with dignity, she thought. Just ask!

"Evelyn, will you tell me something? What... what are they saying about me in town?"

Evelyn cocked her head to one side and gaped at Rachel as if something unusual had passed between them. "Well," she said. "Well! There's the part about you being a pretty young widow. The men grin, the women frown, probably with envy. Then there's the part about you losing your house and refusing help. That made everybody mad. They wanted to help, y'know, to sort of build up Brownie points in case it ever happened to them. Some people have to have help, Rachel, but the next woman to be widowed or go bankrupt is going to feel guilty because you stiffed it out, and she won't be able to. Sort of like you have more backbone. Whoever it happens to be, you won't ever get a kind word out of her. You sure you want to hear this?"

"I can stand it so far."

"When we were in school, you were standoffish, you didn't participate in electives—"

"My mother needed me here."

"What I was getting to was everybody thought after you got that scholarship that we'd never see you again, but you came prancing back to town married to Clive Cameron. I mean, if there was anybody voted most likely to fail!"

Rachel's hand fluttered to her throat. "I didn't know."

"Oh, nobody held it against you. Except maybe Adele. But then, she's always been around the bend. The rest of us, well, when Clive was around we tied everything down. He always had sticky fingers. You were the only one who didn't know it."

The conversation was more basement than bargain. Rachel felt her good humor dissolving like wax near flame. Her brows drew together, her mouth thinned.

"You asked me, Rachel. I thought you really wanted to know."

"I guess I'm not as brave as I thought," she confessed, fumbling in her pocket for a cigarette. She lit it with shaking hands and turned aside to exhale the smoke.

"No one expected you to have clarified vision, y'know, like an artist or something, to home in on the truth. I mean, if you can't trust your husband, who can you trust? Damn! Could I have one of your cigarettes?"

"Oh. Yes. Sorry, I didn't think." She handed over the pack and matches.

"Do you want me to take the children back to town with me?" asked Evelyn disarmingly. "I wouldn't blame you if you did."

"Of course not. I just think I've made a fool of myself trying to protect Clive's good name."

"He was the father of your children so I guess that's obligatory. Any woman would do the same. Why, if Alvin got caught robbing the bank, I'd swear it was the bank's fault for having all that money. And, speaking of Alvin, he's waiting—if you're sure about letting the kids stay."

"I'm positive."

"But, you look so . . . so forlorn."

Rachel forced a smile. "I'll snap out of it." There came a sudden shrill argument from the kitchen. Rachel lifted her hand. "I think I'm wanted to referee the first battle of the day."

"And I'm getting out of here before that changes your mind for sure!" exclaimed Evelyn.

It was minutes later after the squabble over who owned which paper doll was settled that Rachel recalled Evelyn had not said what town talk was concerning herself and Garrett. Then she laughed. Best not to take the lid off that caldron. It might not be so spiritually uplifting.

"What are you laughing at, Mama?"

Rachel glanced at the two girls who were watching her, wide-eyed. "I just thought of a knock-knock joke. Want to hear it?"

Hot dogs, soft drinks and marshmallows were a skimpy beginning. Peanut butter and jelly sandwiches, leftover cake and two gallons of Kool-aid disappeared with alarming speed down insatiable young gullets. Fearing the lining of their stomachs would disintegrate, Rachel sent the youngsters into the garden for more healthy fare. Tomatoes and cucumbers and carrots were inhaled and metamorphosed into energy. Rachel sent a plea heavenward as she stirred sugar into yet another gallon of Kool-aid. Strawberry. Surely God had noticed she had atoned for all of her sins and any that she might commit in the future. He couldn't help but notice, she thought, what with all the yelling and screeching and whooping emanating from the clearing today.

For the visiting youngsters, the small homestead was a windfall to be explored. The sheds out back, the empty pigpen, the chicken coop, all had to be inspected. The lower limbs of every tree encircling the clearing had to be swung from—upside down. The old log spanning the creek had presented a challenge. The fun, of course, being to slip and fall with a big splash. *Fortitude and faith*, Rachel cheered herself on, and went to pick up tennis shoes, socks and shirts that had been discarded about the yard. Seven o'clock would come as it always did every day—only she was wishing desperately that it would arrive far earlier.

Of the children, only Sara and Lily, dangling their feet in the creek, appeared to lag, though their shrill happy voices raised in laughter told Rachel their tiring was her own wishful thinking. The other four kept at their play with utter determination. At least, Rachel mused, she had not had a free moment to grow morose over the letter from the school board or worry about the dwindling reserves of cash.

Gertie Evans arrived on the dot of seven. "Oh, bless her," Rachel breathed as she left the porch and went to greet the tall bony woman. Gertie was thin all over and she had a great beak of a nose that kept one staring past good manners. But beneath her nose was her mouth, which unfailingly wore a ready smile. Rachel liked her.

She and Gertie Evans were lifetime acquaintances, growing friendly when their sons had begun to play together in town, but never becoming close. With a demanding husband, two children and a job in the office of Hollister's Lumber Mill, Gertie never had spare time beyond quick hellos or phone calls to check the whereabouts of her son. Now she appraised Rachel as she stepped from her car.

"From the look of relief on your face, I'd make a guess that you're glad to see me."

"Actually, you're the most beautiful sight in the world," returned Rachel. "And I hope you won't think me ill-mannered if I don't ask you to stay for coffee."

"That bad, eh?"

"Let me put it this way, Gertie. The energy that these six darlings have expended today would light up half of Lackawanna County for a week. Why don't you give a couple of blasts on your horn to get the herd in while I get their clothes. I've got all the discards in a paper sack in the kitchen."

"I think one of the brutes is missing," said Gertie when Rachel returned. She was counting heads and trying to separate the three she was supposed to have in tow.

"Sara," said Rachel, putting the pinch on Caroline. "Go see if your sister's in the bathroom. Tell her to come say goodbye to Lily."

"Sara's not in the bathroom," piped Lily. "She went with Miss Mossy."

"Went where with Miss Mossy?" asked Rachel.

"That way," pointed the child.

Frowning slightly, Rachel followed the direction in which Lily was pointing. "You mean down to the creek?"

The child nodded. "Miss Mossy can't swim, but she can float."

Rachel hurried toward the creek. "Sara!" she called sharply. She raced to the middle of the log, peering up and down the creek. She did not see her daughter.

"Gertie!" she yelled. "Check the house and the bathroom again, will you?" She must be in the bathroom, Rachel thought. Or curled up on her bed. Sara did things like that. Went off to nap without letting anyone know. Gertie emerged from the house, shaking her head.

"She's not here."

Rachel raced back up the path. "Maybe in one of the sheds out back." They all went to look. There was no sign of Sara. She was nowhere to be seen.

"Sara," Rachel whispered through a constricted throat. Her frantic glance took in the clearing, the dark shadowy forest. She separated every tree with her eyes, aching for some brief glimpse of a dark curling halo of hair, tanned chubby legs. Rachel stopped for a heart-beat, then went to stand on the log, once more scruti-

nizing the banks of the creek, darting looks over her
shoulder. She felt herself suspended, thinking . . . she
was right there! Not five minutes ago. How does a child
disappear into thin air? She stared for a moment, dis-
believing. There was no Sara, no Miss Mossy.

"Sara," she cried. "Sara, do you hear me? Answer
Mommy!" *Answer Mommy. Oh, God!*

The silent empty spaces along either side of the creek
shimmered in the heat. A lone frog, prompting dusk,
croaked once and went quiet. Beyond the clearing the
woods rustled, beckoning and cool.

Lurching from the log, Rachel splashed into the
creek, her eyes swiveling in every direction, certain the
next glance would yield Sara's red shirt, her white
shorts.

"Rachel," called Gertie, "I think we'd better phone
for help."

Rachel turned back to face the thin woman. "I don't
have a telephone." She felt sudden dread as though
everything live in her had been bled away.

"I'll go for help, then."

Rachel's breath was short, her answer a shrill sibi-
lant hiss. "Hurry, Gertie. Hurry. It's getting late." Even
as she spoke a dark cloud obscured the departing sun.
The knee-deep water in which she stood felt suddenly
cooler, the rocks and pebbles beneath her espadrilles
slippery and cold, the forest crowding the creek growing dark and menacing. To Pete and Caroline, standing alone, waiflike, she said, "Check the house again.
Look under every bed." She knew it was useless to look.
Sara wouldn't suddenly materialize. "Then stay on the
porch. Don't leave the yard. You hear me?" Panic clot-
ted in her throat.

"What are you going to do, Mom?"

"I'm going down the creek. Sara can't have gone far."
Unless . . .

"Suppose Sara's face went under the water?"

Rachel did not like Caroline voicing her own fears, making them a reality. She began to tremble violently. *Suppose? Suppose!* Unable to answer, she turned away, plunging down the creek bed, leather soles sliding perilously over current-smoothed stone and rock.

At the narrow, sharp bend in the creek she tripped over the submerged fish trap. As she brushed hair and water from her eyes, she caught a sudden movement in the thick underbrush hugging the creek. "Sara!" Clawing her way to the bank, her heart leaped with joy.

The movement growled. Rachel froze. A pair of brown-gold eyes stared at her warily. The animal bared its teeth, fur rising on its neck. Rachel jumped back, feeling her shoe wedge between sharp rocks. Uncaring, with panic at her back like a gale-force wind, she jerked it loose, felt the bone snap. Fear absorbed the pain. An anguished cry of dread issued from her throat. "Sara . . . ! Please, God, please let Sara be all right." Foot dragging, she moved onto the opposite bank and began to crawl.

13

"THAT WAS A STUPID THING to do!" said Garrett, his voice gritty, as he deposited Rachel in the swing on the porch. He had found her a half mile from the clearing. The sight of her, wet and dirty, crawling alongside the creek, calling out weakly for Sara, had weighed down his heart. Her anguish and fear had seeped into him, communicating an urgency he had not known since leaving battle zones in Asia. Pete and Caroline, their faces drawn taut with fright, crowded against the swing. "Pete, get a blanket for your mother. Caroline, a warm washcloth." He knelt before Rachel. "Let me check your foot."

She gazed blankly at Garrett, her face ashen above her torn and stained blouse. She was at the very edge of hysteria. The weight of her fear, the pressure of it, was crushing her bones as surely as if she were miles beneath the sea. "Don't worry about my foot. Find Sara!"

"We will. I've already been a mile up and down either side of the creek. We need help to search. There are gullies and ravines—"

He didn't like to recall the way his gut had wrenched when he had arrived and found Pete and Caroline huddled together on the porch. "Sara's lost, Mommy's gone to find her," they had spoken in unison. He had had to force himself to take the time to radio for help, giving instructions to Slim to gather up the crews from Hollister's Lumber Mill, organize transportation for the inmates, locate Dr. Williams and have the old reprobate collect his mother to watch the children in case he couldn't find Rachel.

As his hands manipulated her ankle, Rachel gasped, yanking him back to the unsettling present. The sound of bone grating on bone was sickening. Garrett let her foot down gently, took the blanket from Pete and wrapped it about Rachel.

"Are you hurt bad, Mommy?" asked Caroline, putting the washcloth in Rachel's hand where it lay limp and dripping. The child's face was puffed up, her eyes swollen from crying.

It was an upward struggle for Rachel to answer her daughter. "No, a little sprain, that's all."

Pete's plain earnest little face was distorted by a worried frown. Garrett put his hand on the boy's shoulder. "Listen, son, why don't you go sit in the cruiser and monitor the radio for me. I'm expecting Deputy Walters to call any minute. Caroline, can you pull a chair out here and prop your mother's foot up?"

When the children had gone to do his bidding, Garrett turned to Rachel. Her eyes swallowed up her face. He almost had to look away. "Now you listen, you've got to get a handle on yourself. You're scaring the wits out of the kids." His voice was clogged and rough. "We'll have forty or fifty volunteers combing these woods in less than an hour. We'll find Sara."

Shadows were growing longer, darker, the surface of the creek beneath the chokecherry looked like shimmering black velvet. Rachel peered anxiously into the gloom. "We can't just stand around waiting! My baby is out there somewhere. She wants me. I know she does. It's getting so dark."

"Listen to me, Rachel. Fearing that something terrible has happened to Sara doesn't make it true. I know you feel it in your gut but your fear is creating its own false sense of reality."

He was bending over her, gripping her shoulders, shaking her, and Rachel couldn't tell if he meant to be shaking. Her whole body was coldly damp and her heart beat with enormous pain.

"She's lost. That's real."

"We'll find her. Believe that." Caroline returned with the chair. Garrett sent her to keep Pete company. It was irrational as hell to be thinking it now, he thought, but passion was easy. Love was hard. Once the idea took hold it didn't seem so irrational; at times like these, love was the glue that held it all together. He could say nothing of this now, for Rachel was whispering desolately into her hands.

"My baby... my baby... oh, what shall I do?"

The small clearing was beginning to fill with cars and trucks and men. Ignoring the hushed pandemonium as they began to emerge from their vehicles and organize into groups, Garrett sat in the swing and took Rachel into his arms. He buried his face into her silky disarrayed hair. "What you can do, Rachel, is pray." He reached back into time, into the jungles of Vietnam for the psalm that had sustained him when he had been a mere boy doing a man's job; for the prayer that had in some way enveloped him in calm, routing his savage fear. "If I ascend to heaven, thou art there. If I make my bed in Seoul, thou art there. If I take the wings of the morning and dwell in the uttermost parts of the sea, even there thy hands shall lead me, and thy right hand shall hold me."

Rachel's quivering stilled. She lifted her eyes to his rugged lined face. "Oh, Garrett, there're so many things about you that I don't know."

"You know everything about me. We'll find Sara and return her to you. Safe. Try not to worry." He gave her shoulder a reassuring squeeze.

"The waiting will be miserable." She reached for his hands as he drew away, seizing them with surprising strength. How deceiving looks can be, she thought, stroking a finger across his knuckles. His were not rough or brutal hands, but tender, gentle, loving.

Hating to do it, Garrett pulled his hands from her grasp. "I have to put this mob to work, Rachel."

She nodded, uneasily afraid, searching deep for the courage and patience she would need to see her through the ordeal, the prayer he had uttered so solemnly haunting her. She could offer none better. *Oh, Sara! Sara! Sara!* she screamed silently.

Garrett spied his mother and Dr. Williams hurrying up the shadowed narrow lane. The clearing was crowded with vehicles, newcomers having to find a parking space on the narrow shoulders of the dusty path. He waved his hat over his head, caught their attention and directed them to Rachel. Searchers stood about in tight little groups, hanging back from the house. Garrett didn't blame them. One look into Rachel's face could make the strongest man feel dread, and guilt that his own children were home and safe. He gave several men he knew curt nods as he passed them on the way to his cruiser. "Anything coming across that radio?" he asked Pete.

"Nothin' yet. Can I go with you to look for Sara?"

"I need you on the radio. Suppose Sara's wandered to the highway and picked up there and taken into town? You'd have to relay the news. Why don't you raise Deputy Walters for me?"

Pete bristled with importance as he handed over the unit.

"Slim," said Garrett when the deputy's voice crackled, "we'll be starting in about twenty minutes. I want a man on the river bridge and I want the mouth of the creek lit up like daylight. That's where we'll rendezvous." He looked at his watch. "About midnight. Pete Cameron will be holding the post here on the radio."

"I copy. I'll be in touch." He cleared his throat. "Sheriff, we got a teletype."

Garrett loosened a groan. "I don't have time for ordinary business, Slim. Put it on my desk. Get cracking on those lights for the river."

"Wait! You've got to hear... It's—you recall that tourist from Alabama that got chewed up by that dog?"

The tone of the deputy's voice caused an icy chill to penetrate Garrett's flesh, enter his soul and dull every sense. "I remember."

"He died... of hydrophobia."

Every bone in Garrett's body turned brittle and heavy. "Confirmed?"

"Yeah, by the State Health Department of Alabama. That's who the teletype is from. Reckon there're any dogs on that mountain?"

Garrett let the hand mike rest in his lap, his eyes fixed trancelike on the milling scene in the clearing. Rabid dogs. *My God!* He turned to Pete. "Where's your sister? I told her to stay with you."

"She was fidgety. She didn't want to sit still."

"Sheriff? You there?"

Garrett put the receiver to his mouth. "Slim, put together the animal control unit. How many of those dart-gun tranquilizers do we have?"

"Two."

"All right. I want two men on the bridge overlooking the creek mouth. If we come on any dogs, we'll herd them that way."

"What's hydrophobia, Sheriff?"

Garrett drew himself up and took a deep breath. "Nothing, Pete, nothing for you to worry about. Why don't you stretch out on the seat and take a nap. It's going to be a long night." Out of the corner of his eye, Garrett spied Caroline in the shadows rounding the trunk of the mulberry tree. She no longer looked like a dark-haired snit, but extremely wan and infinitely fragile.

He approached her, putting his huge hand on her thin shoulder, squeezing gently. "I want you to take care of your mother while we're all out. Can you make coffee, tea or hot chocolate?"

"Yes," she answered in a small voice.

"Then that's what I want you to do. You keep a pot going, because now and again we'll be checking back with you to let you know how the search—how things are progressing. Are you up to it?"

"I'll try."

"Trying isn't good enough. You must be up to it."

The thin young shoulder beneath his huge hand trembled. "I am up to it."

"Good girl. I knew I could count on you. Now, up to the house . . . go on." He considered drawing the reed-thin child into his arms for a moment, but decided against it as he glanced in the direction of the men waiting for him. But the girl's pinched pointed face remained in his mind's eye. He turned back. She had not moved.

"I was thinking I might give you a hug," he said. "One you can pass on to your mother when she's feeling better." With no further ado he scooped her up, and Caroline wrapped her arms about his neck, clinging to him as to a bulwark. "I'm scared for Sara," she said, muffled against his neck.

"Me, too." His taut face and worried eyes affirmed his words. He released her to stand on her own two feet, saying, "But we won't tell your mother that, will we?"

"I can keep a secret."

"You'll be the only woman I know who can," he said dryly, though his smile was kind and accepting.

"I'm not a woman, I'm only seven."

Her slender body shuddered in her vulnerability. Garrett felt his heart contract. He knew himself now as a man whose emotions had not, until today, been deeply touched, but he had plenty of them and a great longing to expend them . . . on Rachel, on Pete, on Caroline and Sara. "You run along now and do like I said. And don't forget your brother in the car. Take him a cup of hot chocolate later on." Garrett watched her for a moment, saw her stumble, catch herself and go on.

A half moon was silvering the sky, and only an owl hooted as he walked across the clearing. Herschel Cutter, bald, stout and overall clad, was just then letting his dogs sniff one of Sara's dolls.

"Cutter," said Garrett softly, "have your dogs been vaccinated against rabies?"

"Yeah, they have," the old man replied. "We got us more'n one problem, Sheriff?"

"Hope not, but it's best to be on the safe side."

"Yeah." Cutter adjusted the tobacco in his mouth with a determined chew.

Garrett took a position on the front steps. Through the screened door he could see into the lighted house. His mother was filling a pot with water, Caroline at her side. Dr. Williams had Rachel sitting on the kitchen table, her leg thrust along its length. Rachel was grimacing. Behind him there came a collective shuffling as the men moved nearer. He turned, trying to focus on the gathering waiting for him to speak. They formed a sea of faces, eager, excited, revved up. He tried to hold his attention on them, but his mind flashed an image of the tourist, and the writhing painful death he must have suffered. He cleared his throat.

"We've got a four-year-old girl child out there. She's mute. Her name is Sara. I want you calling to her softly, no shouting. We'll work in grids, four men to a grid, all the way down the mountain to where the creek meets the river. A deputy will be stationed on the bridge. Check in with him. If we haven't found the child by then, we'll work our way back up. God help the man who doesn't check every inch." Garrett spotted several with rifles resting on a shoulder. "Those of you with guns, take the bullets out. I don't want you shooting each other or the child." Garrett watched heads shoot up, eyes widen as a murmur passed through the crowd. He waited, listening for bolts being shot back, clips and shells being ejected. Satisfied, he nodded.

"All right now, don't try to whistle down any dogs you come on. There's a wild pack that's been ranging over five thousand acres and they've killed a pig on this mountain. You see a dog, you herd it toward the river, if you can. If it's mean, load up and shoot to kill. No head shots. And don't go near it, not even to nudge it with your boot. Animal control will pick up the carcass."

"Haw! Sheriff," shouted a man from the crowd, "you worried that a dead dog is goin' to stand up and nip one of us in our arse?" There was a ripple of laughter. Garrett let it die down.

"If you've been vaccinated against rabies, Amos, you can carry that dog around in your pocket for all I care." Garrett heard a gasp from behind him, then a low keening wail. He called his mother to take Rachel back into the house, then faced the men again. He counted fourteen men in prison whites standing near a deputy. "One county guest in every group," he ordered. "Okay. Let's go!"

Names were called out, teams formed, flashlights snapped on, producing an eerie appearance of sudden pageantry. Then the searchers spread out and began to lope into thick brush. A ghostly unnatural quiet overcame the clearing. The faraway susurrus of wildlife faded beneath the softly called accolade. Sara, Sara, Sara, drifted down the mountain like a leftover echo. Garrett shuddered.

From deep shadows a man in prison garb stepped into the light spilling from the porch. He was young, with a face that went with seeing things and never being surprised. The sheriff started. "What th' hell—"

"Name's Highwater Smith, Sheriff. I can track nigh on as good as any of Cutter's dogs. My granddaddy taught me. He was full-blooded Cherokee."

"What're you in jail for?"

"Gettin' high-handed with folk on a Saturday night."

"Any family?"

"Got a wife. She's fixin' to have a baby."

Garrett studied the lean knowing face. "All right, you work my grid with me. You safe with a gun?"

"Fair to middlin' when I ain't liquored up."

Garrett handed him a key. "Get the shotgun and shells out of the trunk of my patrol car. There's a kid sitting in the front seat, name of Pete. If he's asleep, take him into the house. Mrs. Stark will tell you where to put him. Then meet me across the creek by that fallen log."

Garrett spun on his heel and went in search of Rachel. He found her sitting on the side porch, leaning disconsolately against the wall, knees drawn up and held in place by her arms. "You'd better stay off that foot, Rachel. Sara'll need you lively, not crippled."

"I saw a dog, Garrett. Just past that first turn in the creek. It growled at me. Suppose it . . . suppose it got Sara?"

"Now don't go looking for trouble," he said firmly, though his insides heaved unmercifully.

Rachel stared into the dense dark forest. Her lips trembled. "Sara's never said 'Mommy.' Did you know that?" A sob caught the last word, drowning it out.

Garrett wanted to gather her into his arms, rock her, soothe her, but there was an urgency exploding inside him. He had to move. "I have to go, Rachel."

"I know." She shivered in spite of the warm night air. "What about the dogs, Garrett? Do you think—"

"No! I think no such thing. But they're out there and I wouldn't be doing my job if I didn't give fair warning. That's all."

"Let me go with you."

"You'd only slow us down."

Hysteria burst inside her, loosening fear and anger. "I don't like this," she screamed. "I don't! I don't! I don't!" She pounded her fists on the floor. "I want my baby! I don't want to do nothing!"

Garrett tried to grasp her arms. Rachel squirmed away. "Don't touch me! Don't! Get away from me."

Her anguish seeped into him. He took a step back and hunkered down, balancing himself on one knee. "You just be here when we bring Sara home. You have two other children, they need comforting, they need your reassurances. Rachel . . . we all need you."

She felt herself shrink as her anger oozed away. Her shoulders drooped. "I'm sorry."

"There's nothing to be sorry about." He pulled her to her feet, embracing her, steadying her, trying to hand her in to Dr. Williams who was standing on the threshold listening, eyes downcast. "Go in the house now, let Doc take care of your foot."

"Oh, God, I'm so miserable. I need something to do!"

"I have men waiting."

"Yes," she sobbed. "I want you to go now. I want you to hurry."

"Sheriff Stark?"

Garrett spun about to face a reporter with a portable videotape television camera who thrust a microphone at his chin. "I'm Stark," he confirmed.

"We heard there's a retarded little girl missing and that she's in the same area where a pack of rabid dogs has been prowling. Do you think she's dead?"

Garrett yanked the man up by his shirt so swiftly, so savagely, the reporter came out of his shoes. "Ask another question like that and I'll take your tongue out!"

"Hey, man! I'm only doing my job."

"Vulture! Then do it out of my sight. This is private property. If you're not out by the highway when I get back I'll lock you up for trespassing. Go in the house, Rachel. Stay there until this creep is gone."

Stunned and achingly miserable, Rachel could only think that her life was falling apart again, just like before. Sara had to be safe. *She had to be.*

Once inside the house Rachel's hands dropped limply to her sides. She looked helplessly from Dr. Williams to Martha Stark. "I didn't mean to make a spectacle—"

"You haven't," crooned Martha, taking Rachel's arm. "Anyone can see your heart aches. Come sit down and let Doc Williams put that cast on your ankle. He's got that paste stirred in the pot and if it hardens, why you'll be out a pot."

"It doesn't hurt, really," she protested.

Martha Stark glanced at the doctor and shrugged.

"Look," Dr. Williams said severely. "It doesn't hurt now because I injected it with an anesthetic. But an hour from now it will. And I'm in a bit of a hurry, Rachel. The sheriff wants me at the river bridge when they bring Sara out. You want me to be there, don't you? For Sara?"

"You think Sara's hurt?"

Dr. Williams caught the wild distraught look in her eyes. A signal passed between himself and Martha Stark. Casually, he shepherded Rachel to the kitchen table and helped her onto it. "I do imagine she'll be scraped up a bit, and the mosquitoes are vicious tonight."

"Oh. I have some witch hazel for that."

"Well, good. You can loan it to me." He manipulated the ankle, and began to wrap it in plaster-dipped gauze. When he was finished he stood back, admiring his work. "That'll do until you can come into the clinic. Then I'll put a walker on the heel. Meanwhile, you stay off that foot." Rachel threw him a look, one he had read many times on the faces of harried mothers. "All right, stay off it as much as you can." He helped her from the table to the sofa. Rachel sank down with a weary sigh. To wait.

After Martha Stark saw Dr. Williams to the door, she pulled up a chair and faced Rachel. "You know what I think? First, you need a good strong cup of tea, and after that a bath of sorts. You're a mess."

Rachel looked down at her ragged blouse and mud-spattered shorts. She plucked at a loose button. In her mind's eye she kept picturing the dog glaring at her. She shivered, remembering the stone-cold bloodshot eyes. A gloomy sense of helplessness descended on her. She looked up at Martha Stark, but her eyes refused to focus on the kindly face. After a moment she closed her eyes. "Caroline and Pete?"

"Wiped down and put to bed."

The house was silent, too silent. Sara silent. "I should never have let Lily and Sara stay down by the creek alone." She looked blindly at her hands lying in her lap. She stretched them out, clasping her knees, hard—then harder until her knuckles went white and she began to cry. Martha Stark peeled the fingers from the bruised indented flesh.

14

IT WAS A SMELL SHE KNEW. A good smell, but for some reason her brain, sluggish with sleep, was refusing to identify it. She felt strange, at once deranged and clearheaded. She lay still for a long time before she gave in to the pull of the smell and let it draw her upright on the sofa.

Sitting around the kitchen table were Evelyn Sizemore, Gertie Evans and another woman Rachel couldn't place. But the oddest sight was Adele Cameron hunched over the ironing board running the iron over a piece of waxed paper. *A dream with smells*, thought Rachel. She had never experienced that before. She swung her legs over the sofa, feeling the weight of the cast. She looked at it stupidly for several seconds, then gasped. Oh, dear God! She had slept! While her daughter was... "Sara!"

Startled, the women about the table looked Rachel's way, then in the next instant they were surrounding her. Evelyn was the first to speak. "They haven't found Sara yet—"

"Rachel!" Adele elbowed Evelyn out of her path. Her face was drained of blood. "I didn't mean what I said. I didn't! I don't want you dead. I don't want the children dead! I came as soon as I heard about Sara. They'll find her. They have to, or it'll be my fault. I've been ironing. I always iron when I'm nervous."

Rachel's hands fluttered in the air, as if to slow the gushing torrent pouring from Adele's mouth. The younger women were staring at Adele, aghast.

"Adele!" Evelyn muttered. "My God! You actually said that?"

"Stop! All of you," hissed Rachel. "I don't care what she's said. What are all of you doing here? Where's Martha? What time is it?"

"We put Martha in your bed. She was worn out." Evelyn looked at her watch. "It's just after one A.M. and we're all here because we want to be, we came to help."

"But I don't—"

Evelyn put a hand on Rachel's arm. "You remember what I said earlier? About people wanting to help? We ache for you, Rachel. We're mothers."

"Yes," put in Gertie. "Lily could be out there, with Sara. I felt so guilty when I drove away from here, with my children tucked safely in the back seat. I had to come back." She turned and drew the stranger forward. "This is Slim Walters's wife, Jean. Her mother-in-law is baby-sitting all of our children. Our husbands are out with the searchers. We want to be here, to help you through this—" Whatever else she meant to say seemed to stick in her throat like a fishbone.

Tears streamed down Rachel's face. "I just feel so helpless."

"We do, too," said Evelyn. "But look, we've got this big coffee urn. We made fresh. How about a cup of coffee and then one of us will help you bathe. You're really wild looking, y'know."

"That—thank you," Rachel sobbed.

Gertie began to sniffle.

"Oh, for Pete's sake!" Evelyn blew her nose. "We'll need a wailing wall if this keeps up."

The cast on Rachel's left foot rose to the swell of her calf. She hung it over the rim of the tub and wore a towel for modesty while Evelyn shampooed her hair. Rachel braided it wet.

"You want to wear pajamas or what?" asked Evelyn.

"A skirt and blouse, I think. Just in case..." Her throat tried to clamp shut. "They may take Sara straight to the clinic."

When Evelyn returned with the clothes, she said, "A runner has come in. Young Hollister. They've made it to the bridge and are starting back up the mountain."

Rachel felt leaden, as if the cast enveloped her entire body. "No sign at all? Nothing?"

"Three dogs, that's all. But there are more searchers now. That television crew went on the ten o'clock news. Hollister says about twenty or thirty men were waiting for them at the bridge. And Garrett sent word. Sara isn't in the creek."

"You mean he doesn't think she drowned."

"He's certain. There's a beaver dam clogging the creek on that narrow neck just before it merges with the river." Evelyn hesitated. "That's where they found her doll."

"They found Miss Mossy?" Rachel's heart leaped with hope.

"Just the doll. Garrett is speculating that Sara's curled up somewhere and gone to sleep."

Rachel clenched and unclenched her fists. "If only she could talk! I wish—"

"Right now isn't the best time to trail out the past and hindsight. Save it until it counts, I always say."

Rachel tried smiling. "You're keeping my mind off the bad things, Evelyn. Thanks. How did we miss becoming good friends, anyway?"

"Oh, kids, husbands, dishes and diapers, narrow little worlds of our own. Hey! We'd better get back to the kitchen, or everyone will think we've both drowned." She made a little moue, a cross between wonder and vexation. "I wish I'd known how Adele handles her nerves, I could've brought my ironing out!"

"Hindsight," said Rachel and hobbled out of the bathroom. The odor of damp was in the air. Rachel stopped and looked at the sky. Stars and moon were no more than a dull glow behind black clouds. Don't let it rain, she pleaded, not yet, not until Sara is safe in my arms. "I can't wait to feel Sara's silky skin," she said as Evelyn held the screened door open for her.

For Rachel the night passed. Not in minutes and hours, for the hands on the clock did not appear to move, but in the ebb and flow of conversation. Or the heart-stopping instances when runners emerged from the forest. At these times, she braced herself for the worst, then sagged with a sickening feeling in her stomach at the news that Sara had not yet been found.

And after the runner had disappeared into the darkness again, she was plagued with images of Sara: her tanned round face, the way her cap of dark curls bounced, the wide eyes that told so much and so little. She could be scared. She could be in danger. These last images were always so overwhelming that Rachel literally ached for the sight of Sara. The throbbing in her ankle was an extension of the pain—ever present like the panic that swelled within her and made her want to bellow for help.

Adele had long since given up ironing and now lay on the sofa, "just to close my eyes a minute." Her snores rose and abated, a truncated rhythm. At the table Evelyn and Gertie rested, heads lying on folded arms. Jean

Walters, rinsing cups at the sink, smiled slightly at Rachel.

"We could sit on the porch for a while, if you want."

Rachel nodded and went out. "I'm scared it's going to rain."

They both looked at the sky. The dark scudding clouds had more substance, appeared heavy, bloated, ready to burst. "I know it's harrowing for you," said Jean hesitantly.

"It is," admitted Rachel. "You worry that something might happen to your kids, but you don't actually believe it will. I'm still . . . I was looking right at her! Then Gertie drove up and my back was turned five minutes. It just doesn't seem possible that five minutes—" She stopped to swallow.

"Come sit down," Jean coaxed, touching Rachel on the shoulder. "Let's swing."

Rachel rubbed her eyes with her fingers. "Oh, God! I just want my life to be back to normal."

"It will be," Jean said quickly. "You just wait and see."

"It's the waiting . . ."

"That's why we're all here."

"I know." Rachel was perilously close to tears again. "I'm thankful for everything, for all—I wish . . ." She wished Garrett was next to her in the swing. She wished for his strength, for his assurances. . . . She felt a tightening in her chest. She needed him badly. He was out there, looking for her little girl. She had treated him terribly, concerned about his reputation, concerned about her own. Such little things. Microscopic. You couldn't even see them with the naked eye. When he brought Sara home, she would hug him, after she'd seen to Sara. Kiss him, right in front of the entire world. Tell him she loved him. She thought about how tough he was on the outside, how tender inside. A smile lifted the corners of her mouth.

Jean saw and wisely remained silent.

The night wind blew and with it came a misting rain.

"Throw this sweater over your shoulders," said Gertie, taking the place beside Rachel that Jean had vacated. "And I've brought you coffee. Though I think by morning we're all going to be freaked out on caffeine."

"If morning ever comes," murmured Rachel bleakly.

Gertie patted her knee. "It will and then they'll find Sara. They won't be able to miss her red shorts."

"Shirt. Red shirt," corrected Rachel.

"Would you like to take a nap?" ventured Gertie. "I can get Martha up. Evelyn's lying down beside her. And Jean's crashed in Sara's bed in the loft. You don't mind, do you?"

Rachel wanted to say she did mind. Using Sara's bed was as if they were closing up the gap left because Sara wasn't there. Filling all the spaces. Baby spaces, four-year-old spaces. *Oh, God! Sara, please be alive.* "I'm not at all sleepy," she answered. "I just want it to be tomorrow."

Gertie was unable to force her usual smile. "It'll be light in an hour."

Time was stagnant. Rachel felt that her very nerves were seeping from her pores, leaking out of her body to join the rivulets of water dripping from the roof. She sipped on the coffee and smoked a cigarette. "Gertie, I don't want you to think . . . I'd like to be alone for a while. I feel so—"

"I understand. I need to freshen up anyway."

Rachel watched Gertie go into the house, then closed her eyes. She purged her mind, emptying it, making it ready to accept—whatever it was that she would have to.

Dawn, when it came, was a gray unhurried event made even more dull by the steadily falling rain. It was quiet now. Crickets were silent. Chickens came down from their wet roosts and huddled, heads together beneath drooping brush. The clearing was deserted.

A movement in the forest, merging into shadows, caught Rachel's eye. She snapped alert, staring at the spot. Nothing. She moved quietly from the swing to the end of the porch, taking care that the cast did not clump, fearing the noise would chase the elusive movement. "Sara?" Her voice was hoarse and didn't carry.

Sirens shattered the stillness. Rachel froze. Listened.

The five women burst from the house and surrounded Rachel. "What is it?"

"I don't know."

"They're not coming here," said Evelyn, wiping sleep from her eyes. "It's dying out."

"Here they come!" Gertie said excitedly.

"Here they come! Rachel! They've found Sara. That must be—"

The women on the porch all turned to watch the searchers straggling into the yard. The men smiled wearily, gave thumbs-up signals or touched their hats before angling toward their cars and trucks. They appeared strangely subdued and none spoke. Car doors slammed, motors revved and started.

Heart hammering, Rachel looked about wildly. "Wait! Wait! Where's—"

Then she saw the man in prison garb emerge from the forest. He had a jacket-wrapped bundle clasped to his chest.

Rachel clung to the porch railing for support. "Sara?"

The inmate smiled as he approached the porch. "She's wet and hungry—"

Rachel grabbed the bundle, threw back the jacket and gazed at her daughter. She ran a finger down the grimy lovely insect-ravaged cheek. She thought she said thank-you, but the commotion was great. Laughter. Tears. See? I told you they'd find her. Everything's fine now. Damn, why am I crying? Somehow they were all in the kitchen, with the sleeping child on the table, while Rachel pressed her head to Sara's heart. "Oh, she's alive. She's alive."

The man who had brought her home was standing by the sink, out of the way, sipping coffee pressed on him by Martha Stark who was mortified that in the excitement, her long white braids had slipped their pins. Rachel looked at the young knowing face and when their eyes met, she smiled.

Sara stirred as they washed her, laughed over her. Her eyes fluttered open. "Hi, Mommy."

"Hi, darling."

Hi, Mommy.

"The dogs didn't like me. I had to climb a tree."

"You did?" Rachel couldn't take her eyes from the rosebud mouth. Sara lisped slightly. The chills came, the aftershock. Joyous warmth swelled within Rachel. She wanted to put her arms around her daughter and hold on to her forever.

Sara was fed and put to bed. The commotion in the loft awakened Pete and Caroline. Breakfast was prepared. The tale of the rescue was elicited from a reluctant Highwater Smith. He told of finding Sara clinging to the low branch of a lightning-struck tree. Rachel's mind was on Sara, and it was only when Martha Stark spoke that she jerked to attention.

"We heard the sirens. Was somebody hurt?"

Highwater Smith hedged.

"You were with the sheriff, weren't you?" asked Rachel.

"It was the dogs, ma'am," said the inmate without looking at Mrs. Stark. "There was a den of 'em. A bitch with pups. Between us and the girl. She wasn't up to keeping her balance much longer so the sheriff waded into 'em."

"And?" prompted Gertie when the man seemed uninclined to say more.

"He got chewed up a bit."

"A bit or bad?" Rachel could barely get the question out of her mouth.

"Were they rabid?" asked Martha, her face going pale.

"Ma'am," the inmate began, "all I know is the doc checked the girl and told me to tote her home and then he worked over the sheriff some and they went off toward the bridge and I came here."

"What about the dogs?"

"Animal control's got 'em. I've said more'n I was supposed to."

"Somebody's got to drive me into town," announced Martha. "Right now."

Evelyn looked at Rachel. "Everything's under control here?" Rachel could only nod. "Good. Martha, get your purse. Gertie and I and Jean'll see you to the clinic."

"What about you?" Gertie said to Highwater. "You need a lift back to the jail?"

"No'm. The sheriff gave me furlough until my wife has her baby or I git drunk, whichever comes first. Mr. Hollister is picking me up. He said to wait here. If'n it's okay with you?" he amended, addressing Rachel.

"*Were* the dogs rabid?" Rachel held her breath. She felt a little dizzy. Adele was in the nook making the bed, the other women were crowding out the door, but they all stopped, listening for Highwater's reply.

"They were mean. That's all I could tell. But they never got to your girl. The doc made certain before he let me bring her home."

Once the carload of women had driven off down the lane, Adele took command with a kind of vigor uncharacteristic of her. Highwater Smith was shooed onto the porch along with Pete to keep him company. Caroline went back to the loft to watch over Sara. Rachel was torn between staying with her family and racing off to the hospital to find out how Garrett fared. But she didn't want to let her children out of sight. "When Sara wakes up, I want to go into town," she told Adele.

"You can't drive with that foot."

"I'll manage."

"I can drive you. Why don't you get some rest now?"

"Sara might wake up and need me."

"That's where I went wrong as a mother," said Adele. "I made sure Clive would need me—no matter what."

"There's a difference, Adele. Sara is only four."

"That's when it starts. I never let go." Adele's face crumpled, but she held herself rigid. "If I hadn't been the way I was, Clive might be alive today. I guess I made him miserable, and you, too. And myself," she added, a revelation that made her eyes widen.

"Adele, let's just remember the good times, for the children's sake."

Rachel's emotions, after all the excitement, were plummeting. She felt physically and mentally wiped out.

She fought her instinct, which was to go to Garrett's side that minute. What she'd thought, hoped, planned was that Garrett would return Sara, and then they would live happily ever after. Fairy tales. Life wasn't a fairy tale. And she wasn't overprotective. If she had been, the entire horror of Sara's being lost would never have happened.

"Mr. Hollister's here," said Pete, poking his head in the door.

Hollister was lanky, wizened and weary from tramping about the rain-damp mountain the night before. He greeted Rachel with, "How's that scamp of a girl of yours this morning?"

"Unlike the rest of us," said Rachel, smiling, "she's hardly the worse for wear. I want to thank—"

"We were glad to help," he said quickly, brushing away her thanks. Then he cleared his throat. "I know maybe this ain't the time, but I've always been one to get on to a thing I've decided about."

Puzzled, Rachel stared at the man. "Decided about?"

"Well, clomping through that brush last night I couldn't help but notice you got a powerful amount of pine ready to be cut. Some of the young growth is gettin' fair choked out. And that ain't healthy."

"You want to chop down my trees?"

"Not all of 'em. It's what we call selective harvesting. Clear out the overgrowth—the tall 'uns. Then fifteen, twenty years from now, you'd have another good stand, healthy, too. I thought to offer you five thousand dollars to let me work ten acres beginning, say, a thousand yards down White Hawk Creek."

Five thousand dollars! Rachel was too stunned to answer.

Hollister's eyes narrowed. "Seven thousand, then, and I'd throw in enough board feet for you to do any repairs you want on this place. That's my top offer."

Rachel's heart was stopping more than it was beating.

"That's the best I can do, Miz Cameron, what with all the laws we got. Cost me money to clean up behind the cuttin' crews to prevent erosion." He drew a rough hand through his sparse hair. "Fact is, everything is done scientific nowadays. Don't do nothin' but cost a man money."

"I understand what you're up against, Mr. Hollister." Her voice was shaking. "Seven thousand dollars and the board feet are acceptable."

"Well! You can pick up the check next time you're in town. Just call at the mill." He said goodbye to Adele, and signaled Highwater Smith to his truck.

"Wait!" Rachel called.

Hollister's expression was guarded, as if he thought Rachel had changed her mind about the trees. "Mr. Hollister, have you heard anything about Sheriff Stark? How bad he's hurt?"

"He just needed some sewing up. His legs. I reckon the dogs got the worst of it. Stark's hide's tougher'n leather. Oh, I 'most forgot. Deputy Walters said he'd send somebody for the sheriff's car."

Rachel exhaled air that she'd been holding in her lungs.

"I never thought about a tree being worth money," said Adele, slightly awed.

"Me, either," replied Rachel, looking past Adele, seeing into the future. Seeing meat on the table every night for dinner. Seeing her children in pristine new school clothes, seeing cavities repaired and new tires on the old station wagon. Thoughts were too much. Suddenly weary beyond measure, she hobbled to her bed. "I think I will take a nap now, but you'll wake me when Sara gets up?"

"As soon as I hear a squeak," promised Adele.

"Then we'll go into town." Rachel sank down on the bed and closed her eyes. "I want to see Garrett," she whispered. See him, touch him, hold him, love him— and pray that the dogs weren't rabid.

15

"DID YOU SAY anything mean to her?"

"Rachel . . . no! I told you I was sorry for before. Caroline told me she was awake. I went up to her and said, 'Hi, sleepyhead' and she just looked at me and turned over. That's all. After a minute she got up and went to the bathroom, but she hasn't said a word to Pete or Caroline, either." Adele looked as tired as Rachel felt, and now distraught.

"Well, maybe she's just fatigued," ventured Rachel. But she wasn't sure. Perhaps only the trauma of being lost, then found had loosened Sara's tongue for those few joyous moments. Perhaps Adele's presence, though, was a contributing cause to Sara's being silent again. Rachel sighed. "I think I'll drive the station wagon myself, Adele. You can follow behind and if I have any trouble—"

"If you're sure."

"Yes. I'll stop by the clinic, too. With a walker on this cast, I should manage just fine. And I really don't need my left foot to drive."

"STAND UP ON THAT," Dr. Williams ordered as he helped Rachel from the table. "How's it feel?"

"A little wobbly."

"It'll take some getting used to. But I warn you, if you don't stay off your feet, that ankle is going to give you trouble from here on out."

"I'll try," Rachel said to appease him. "What room is Garrett Stark in? I'd like to step in and say hello."

"He isn't here, he went on down to Little Rock."

"The capital? But, why? They told me—" Her voice barely worked. "He was injured really bad, then?"

"His legs were torn some and he lost a lot of blood. We sewed him up here, gave him a transfusion, but I think he accompanied the dogs to the State Health Department."

"To find out if they had rabies?"

"And to pick up the vaccine if he needs to take the shots."

Rachel's hands felt clammy and hot. "I see. Do you know when he'll be back?"

Dr. Williams shrugged. "He could be a while. They pulled eight dogs out of those woods. Takes time to do the tests. Why don't you ask at the station. They'd know more."

"Dr. Williams, I get the impression that you know something you're not telling me."

"There is such a thing as a patient's privacy."

"What does that mean? What's wrong with Garrett?"

"Nothing that he won't recover from, and that's all I can say."

Rachel collected the children from the waiting room where they'd been entertained by the receptionist. Outside the clinic in the rain-washed air her chest heaved, expanding as she caught her breath.

"What are we going to do now, Mom?"

Rachel ruffled Pete's hair. She told them about the sale of timber. "We're going to get a telephone."

"What about a television?"

"A television, too. A small one."

"In color?"

"We'll see." She looked down at Sara. So sweet, so small, so quiet. *Dear God. Please. I want her to babble, shout, shriek and—lisp. Do that for me, please.*

At the sheriff's office they had no news of Garrett. He had only been gone since noon. As Rachel parked beneath the mulberry tree it seemed incredible it had only been yesterday that calamity had struck. And tonight their lives were returning to some semblance of order.

They had been home twenty minutes when a car drove up. *Garrett!* Rachel put dents in the wooden floor with her new metal heel in her haste to get to the front door.

"Mrs. Cameron?"

"Yes. Who're you?" she asked of the short slender man who had a receding hairline, which he tried to camouflage by combing his hair forward.

"I'm Bradbury, with WNET News." He threw up a hand. "Please, hear me out. Look, we've got a shot of you and the sheriff and the searchers, one of the sheriff being loaded into an ambulance, and we know your daughter has been found. We'd like a shot of her. People want to see her, sort of a happy ending."

Rachel hesitated. "I don't want any notoriety."

"Just a picture, that's all."

"Our picture would be in the paper?" asked Caroline, beginning to preen.

"Probably. On television, for sure."

"I don't want to be in it," said Rachel. "I'd let you do it if you just took the children. All the children."

The reporter smiled. "I'll get my cameras."

When he returned to the house, Sara squealed, "Miss Mossy! Miss Mossy!" She grabbed the still sodden doll from Bradbury's hand and began to chastise the doll for getting lost.

"I think I'm a hit," said the reporter. "I picked the doll up on the bridge. I guess in all the confusion, it got left behind."

Rachel didn't want to explain about Sara's silences, but it seemed as if she were being handed another miracle. And Bradbury got all the pictures he wanted, including one of Rachel.

Later when she tucked Sara into bed, she said, "Don't you ever give me the silent treatment again, you little scamp. I worry."

"I was only pouting," said Sara.

"The next time you only pout, I might only spank!"

DAYS WENT BY. Rachel picked up the check from Hollister's mill. The television, color, was bought, although too late to see themselves when the rescue films were aired. But Rachel bought six newspapers in which their pictures were on the front page. Each of the children had to have his own, and they became minor celebrities among their pint-sized acquaintances. The lumber crews had begun to work the forest. The telephone was installed. Rachel talked on the telephone to Evelyn and Gertie and Martha, always saving Jean Walters for last. "No, Slim hasn't heard from the sheriff, but soon. He'll call you." But Slim never did.

One morning Rachel was hanging the wash on clotheslines in the backyard. When she peeked over a sheet to check on Sara in the garden, there stood Garrett. They stared at one another as if they were two strangers in a foreign country and the only means of communication was the lifting and lowering of eyebrows.

Garrett had on a pair of dark tweed slacks and a striped oxford cloth shirt. His old hat appeared to have acquired some vigor, for the brim bent low and stayed there. He looked wonderfully suave.

Something had happened to Rachel's tongue. It refused to form a syllable. She rubbed her hands down the sides of her shorts. Her old shorts, the ones with the hanging hems. She must look awful! And Garrett looked beautiful. It wasn't fair.

"Has that cast taken root? Or can you stump over here and say hello?"

"Why didn't you call first? Why didn't you call—" Oh, damn! She could feel her eyes swelling, tears forming.

"Hey, now." He stepped around the sheet, moving stiffly and with an economy of motion.

Rachel glared at him. "Don't you touch me!"

"Ever?"

"Maybe not ever—oh, I've been so worried about you and nobody would tell me anything and I've made a fool of myself pestering the folk in town and at your office."

"Fed the gossip, did you?"

"Why are you walking like that?"

"I've got stitches from my ankles to my fanny."

Rachel sagged, beginning to feel ashamed of her outburst. Beginning to, but not entirely. "Now you're trying to make me feel bad. But you should've called me. I even went to the clinic to see you. You weren't there."

"Smile at me, Rachel. I've been thinking an awful lot about the way you smile. That got me to dreaming about your lips . . ." He reached for her.

"I'm all sweaty."

"I love your sweat."

"But you're all clean and handsome."

"I'm glad you think so." His arms were around her, his hand running lightly up her spine. "Thinking of this kept me sane," he murmured, and began a series of tiny kisses on her mouth, her eyes, her cheeks, her brow.

Rachel felt his swelling erection against her thighs. Garrett groaned and there was something in the sound that made Rachel lean back and look at his face. "Garrett, did you . . . I mean—" Her gaze dropped to the juncture of his thighs. "You're hurt down there, aren't you?"

Blood rushed to his cheeks. "Just nipped."

"How many nips?"

"Ten stitches' worth."

"But, how can we—?"

"Actually, we can't, at least not for a week or so."

Sara peeked around the sheet. "Hi, theriff."

Garrett stepped away from Rachel. "Hi, sport. You been tramping around the woods while I've been gone?"

"No. If I did, I'd get a spankin'. Have you been huggin' my mommy?"

"Don't answer that," Rachel ordered.

"We have a TV, a phone and theven dollars," continued Sara, undaunted.

"We also don't have any secrets around here anymore," said Rachel. "The only time we get any peace and quiet is when she's pouting. Which isn't near often enough, and I never thought I'd live to see the day when I'd tell her to shut up."

Garrett laughed. "I'm glad she's fine and that you are, too. I missed you, Rachel."

Her eyes shone. "In the house, both of you. I'll fix us a cool drink."

"Not Kool-aid," suggested Garrett.

"For you, a beer."

"Beer! You have moved up in the world."

Rachel had changed into a skirt and blouse and as she settled in the swing next to Garrett, she tucked the folds about her legs. The children watched television in the house, giving the adults the illusion of privacy. For a few minutes she and Garrett maintained a friendly comfortable silence. But the quiet soon became awkward. Rachel drew in a quavering breath. "Tell me about the dogs," she said. "And I think you owe me an explanation of why you haven't been in touch."

"I wanted to make sure the test on the dogs for rabies was thorough, so I stayed in Little Rock. None had rabies, thank God."

"But that tourist?"

"It was his own dog that bit him. She was diseased. The idiot who sent us the information failed to mention that. The telex was just an alert in case any of us had come in contact with his dog. None of us had."

"That doesn't explain why you stayed away from me."

"I didn't plan it, if that's what you mean. But it did cross my mind that I might end up only half—" Even now it was too much to contemplate. "Being a woman, you wouldn't understand. When a man gets an injury to his privates . . . Well, hell! I was terrified."

"That doesn't say very much for me. I could've helped you!"

"I don't think so. Doc Williams said no sexual excitement. Around you, I get excited."

"Are you in much pain?"

"Not now. It hurt like hell when the stitches came out."

"I can imagine." She watched a spider spin a thread that carried it from roof beam to porch railing.

"A week's a long time."

Rachel sighed. "It is, isn't it."

He took a cigar from his pocket, peeled the cellophane from it, inspected it, bit off the end, inspected it again. "Hate to waste a whole damn week. I was wondering if you'd noticed Caroline and I are getting along?"

"She hasn't said anything, but I thought you might be. She spent a day looking for a pencil with an eraser so she could rub out 'horridest' in her diary."

Garrett's eyes narrowed, indignant. "She called me that?"

"I thought it was rather mild, considering."

"But wholly undeserved!"

Rachel flashed him one of her more flamboyant smiles. "You think so?"

"I'm nice. Don't you think I'm nice?"

"I think you're one of the most stubborn, hard-headed men I've ever known. And very brave."

Garrett's cheeks turned pink and he tried to camouflage the blush by puffing hard on his cigar. Rachel wanted to touch him, to lean against him, feel his warmth and ropy muscles, but she didn't dare. The week they must wait suddenly seemed to loom as the chasm of time between birth and death—a lifetime! "Are you back at work now?" she asked.

"Just to clear up some desk work and give a few orders. Deputy Walters has things under control."

"I like his wife, Jean."

"Speaking of wives," Garrett began, but his heart tripped. Damn! In his mind it had seemed the easiest thing in the world to ask a woman. Now he wasn't certain.

An arc of excitement shot through to the very marrow of Rachel's bones. "You were saying?"

Garrett's gaze found the busy spider. He studied it intently. "I've been thinking about getting married."

"Really?" said Rachel.

"I'm thirty-eight, y'know. About time I settled down. What do you think?"

"I think it's a wonderful idea."

Insects hummed, mingling with the buzz of saws of the timber crews that came faintly on the breeze into the clearing. Garrett turned to Rachel, his light-colored eyes somber, his expression one of relief. "I'm glad that's done."

"Who're you going to marry?" she asked.

"Who? What kind of question is that? You just agreed with me."

"What did I agree to?"

"You're being spiteful."

"I just want to know who you're marrying. One of the waitresses at Nester's?"

"Hell, no! You! I'm marrying you!"

His shouting brought the children to the screened door. Rachel attempted to shoo them back to the television, but they wouldn't have it.

Pete spoke. "You're going to marry my mom?"

"I saw them hugging," snickered Sara.

"You won't have any place to sleep," announced Caroline.

Garrett pursed his lips like a petulant child. Then he roared. "This is grown-up business. Back into the house, all of you!"

Pete grinned and took Sara's hand. "Yessir."

Caroline lingered at the door. "Will you take us to the beach?"

GARRETT LAY stretched on the sand on Galveston Beach watching Rachel out of the corner of his eye. She wore a one-piece swimsuit that fit her admirably. So admirably that he felt pangs of jealousy when strolling men gave her a second glance. Her golden tan contrasted sharply with the cast on her ankle. "You're not sorry, are you?"

She was gently tracing the new scars on his legs with a finger. "Why would I be sorry?"

"Because we haven't . . . you didn't have a wedding night."

She smiled impishly. "We've made good use of the week, though, haven't we? We had a nice ceremony, ordered a room built onto the house. Got your stuff moved— Oh, here come Adele and your mother with the children."

"How are you two honeymooners?" said Martha with a smile as she shook out a towel under a nearby umbrella.

"We're fine." Rachel eyed her brood as they raced to the water's edge with Adele, looking uncommonly frazzled, following behind them. "The kids wearing you two out?" she asked of Martha.

"Not me, but they convinced Adele to ride down the water slide." Martha shook her head. "I didn't have the courage. We're all about ready for a nap. What about you two?"

Rachel looked at Garrett. "Are we?"

He trailed a finger down her spine, causing goose bumps to erupt on her arms and legs. "I think so."

An hour later, swathed in a robe, Rachel lay on the bed in the suite she and Garrett shared, her ankle propped up on pillows. She was thinking how lucky she was. How happy. She was loved. Her children were healthy, her finances were in good order for the first time in her life. Better than good, she amended thoughtfully, recalling the evening that Garrett had told her about his pension from the Marines. Over a thousand dollars a month and he had been banking it for two years. He had had to drag out his savings book to convince her. And then came the notice from social security. Checks for the children would begin arriving in September and, wonder of wonders, they would be retroactive from the day she had first filed. It wasn't much, only forty dollars each, but Garrett agreed that the money could be banked for their education.

He had balked, though, at her acceptance of the subbing job. She took it anyway. Not so much for the money, but because it established her independence. Married to a man as strong-willed as Garrett, a little independence went a long way. She never wanted to suffer that closed in, nowhere-to-turn feeling again.

Her husband was still in the shower when the children burst in through the connecting door. "Can we watch television in here?" asked Pete.

"For a few minutes," agreed Rachel.

"No!" said Garrett, coming out of the bathroom with a towel wrapped about his middle.

"Why not?" questioned Caroline, making herself comfortable on the foot of the big bed.

"Because there's some little something your mother wants me to do for her. Out, all of you." He shepherded them into the rooms they shared with their grandmothers, then locked the door.

"Some little something?" Rachel said throatily after Garrett threw off the towel and lay beside her.

"Get naked," he ordered, his breath coming short, "and I'll show you."

Rachel felt him growing hard against her. She hesitated, and then reached down to touch his maleness. "Are you certain it'll be all right?"

"It won't be if you keep your hand there," he groaned.

"Does it hurt to get all stretched out like that?"

"Aches something fierce," he whispered, taking her into his arms. He trailed kisses across her eyelids, gently forcing them closed.

"Why don't you stop, then?"

"Because the ache is for you. I want you. I love you . . ." His hands explored, discovered and mapped her silken flesh. He kissed her mouth, ran his lips down her neck and fastened onto a nipple. Tiny thundering sensations began to sweep over her.

She moved to caress him, guiding him into her slowly, with care, listening for the telltale gasp that meant pain to him instead of pleasure. But the only sounds from him were those of exaltation and the bonds of restraint were swept away. Rachel lost track of everything around her except the pulse beating in her ears.

Their release was one of pure incoherent joy.

Rachel lay utterly relaxed alongside Garrett, one arm flung across his chest. She could feel his heartbeat subsiding, returning to normal. "Do you think it will always be this way between us?" she asked in a whisper, for she did not want to destroy the lovely languorous mood that embraced them both.

"Not like this, no. Better."

"Better would be impossible."

"Better, because I can come home to you every day. Lie with you every night, hold you, touch you. Talk with you...make love to you. You do like making love, don't you?"

Her eyes locked with his, conveying the answer.

"Could you come a little closer and show me?"

"Of course."

"And be careful with that cast! You've just about destroyed my shinbones."

"Did you have to say that? Couldn't you be romantic, just this once?"

"If you ask me nicely."

Rachel smiled, gathered herself and mounted him, taking an inordinate amount of time to position herself. "How is this for nice?"

"I can feel myself getting romantic."

She leaned forward and kissed him on the mouth. "So can I..."

THE AUTHOR

Jackie Weger didn't discover her gift—a genuine talent for writing romance—until four years ago. Before that, she was too busy being the working mother of five children. We may have had to wait a while for Jackie, but it was worth it.

Wings of Morning is Jackie's fourth Harlequin Temptation. As with all her books, its unique flavor is the result of on-site research, and characters that go on living after the story ends.

Harlequin Temptation

COMING NEXT MONTH

#93 SLOW MELT Jane Silverwood

The moment Kate met Chris in a change room, she realized he was exceptional. Even with his clothes *on*, she wanted to see more and more of him....

#94 A WEEK FROM FRIDAY Georgia Bockoven

Repossessing a man's car was one way to earn money—and guaranteed to disenchant the owner. Yet when Eric caught Janet in the act, he was anything but turned off....

#95 STAR-CROSSED Regan Forest

Living together for fourteen days in the wild made them friends. Sharing fourteen nights under a canopy of stars made them lovers. But sharing a lifetime seemed no more than a dream....

#96 WITHOUT PRECEDENT JoAnn Ross

Jessica was a divorce lawyer, and highly skeptical about happy ever afters. Which was just what Quinn had in mind for them....

Take 4 novels and a surprise gift FREE